MASTERS
of
ILLUSION

MASTERS
of
ILLUSION

Mary-Ann Tirone Smith

WARNER BOOKS

A Time Warner Company

FIC
SMI

15324

Warner Books, Inc., 1271 Avenue of the Americas, New York, NY 10020

 A Time Warner Company

Printed in the United States of America
First Printing: June 1994
10 9 8 7 6 5 4 3 2 1

Library of Congress Cataloging-in-Publication Data
Smith, Mary-Ann Tirone.
    Masters of illusion : a novel of the Connecticut circus fire/
Mary-Ann Tirone Smith.
        p.   cm.
    ISBN 0-446-51806-9
    1. Hartford Circus Fire, Hartford, Conn., 1944—Fiction.
2. Ringling Brothers Barnum and Bailey Combined Shows—History—Fiction.   3. Circus—
Connecticut—Hartford—History—20th century—Fiction.   4. Fires—Connecticut—
Hartford—History—20th century—Fiction.   5. Hartford (Conn.)—History—Fiction.   I.
Title.
PS3569.M537736M37   1994
813'.54—dc20   93-6320
                                                                                                        CIP

Book design by Giorgetta Bell McRee

This book is dedicated to my beloved Tirone cousins:

*Jack, Bobby, Kathy, Jule-Ann, Dee Dee, Frank, Tommy, Paul,
Wally, Elaine, Sandy, Barbara and Jimmy.*

And to my equally beloved Deslauriers cousins:

*Ernie, Moe, Francis, Paul, Doris, Juney, Donny, Cleasse, Roger, Ruthie,
Billy, Rita, Richard, Rusty, Joe, Matt, Ray, Marietta and Greg*

And in precious memory of:

Beezie, Jackie, Karen and Michael.

ACKNOWLEDGMENTS

I would like to acknowledge the enthusiastic assistance of the reference departments of the Hartford and Danbury Public Libraries, and the boundless support of the staff of the Ridgefield Library.

MASTERS
of
ILLUSION

Chapter One

Margie Potter had a scar on her back, the thumbprint of a soldier on liberty who had passed her along the line of a bucket brigade. A bucket brigade of sorts. The actual bucket brigade—a dozen roustabouts plus Emmett Kelly the clown and two neighborhood women—passed their buckets of water from hand to hand just to give themselves something to do. But it was almost all military men in Margie Potter's bucket brigade, soldiers waiting with their orders at Brainard Field in Hartford for the transport that would take them to Europe. Those furloughed on July 6 took a bus over from the field to enjoy the matinee performance of the Greatest Show on Earth. They were young, and so they'd chosen to come into town to the circus rather than head out for the nearest gin mills. Other than the soldiers, there were few men in the tent, instead, only women and children and a few grandfathers who'd already served in the first war.

Six thousand people fled the burning tent, and now they stood in the lot, stock-still, horrified. And what was so strange was that, in the news photos, all those people standing stock-still were facing *away* from the tent. Fires were supposed to have something to do with thrills and sex; people's eyes are irresistibly drawn to flames, but not this day. The fire that consumed the biggest circus tent in the world (three city blocks long) in less than six minutes meant only death and destruction. Unspeakable, just like that the war, but without hope of victory. Also unspeakable was that the war, in a way, was responsible for the fire. When the Ringling brothers constructed their new tent, they had had no access to waterproof canvas. The War Department needed all there was. So the clever roustabouts figured out how to waterproof the tent themselves: They mixed up a solution of one part softened paraffin to two parts gasoline, and when they got it to the consistency of mayonnaise, they painted their canvas with it.

The soldiers formed a line leading from the wild animal chute running parallel to the main entrance to a place beyond the titanic heat where the ambulances would arrive, eventually. It was a "short" lot, the circus term for inadequate, and so the ambulances couldn't get past the sideshow and food stands and all the trailers for many hair-raising minutes.

After the men had managed to save about two dozen people, the first man in the line (the only one who wasn't military) had to make a wretched decision—when to quit. He was Hermes Wallenda, the youngest of the Flying Wallendas, the troupe of tightrope performers whose lives were full of wretched decisions. Twenty years after the circus fire, when the seven-man pyramid collapsed under the big top in Detroit, it was Hermes who announced at a press conference that the survivors would go on with the show the next evening, though two of the family were dead and one severely injured.

The men passed along burned, mostly unconscious, or shocked children, handed to them by their mothers up and over the metal rungs of the chute that barred their intended route to the wide entrance where they'd poured in just twenty minutes earlier, babbling with anticipation.

There was no way to save the mothers.

After Hermes made his decision, the men ran for their lives.

People had spread blankets for the injured children to lie on while waiting for the ambulances to come. Those people bent over the victims, arms outstretched, trying to shade the seared bodies from the hot afternoon sun. They waited and waited, and then they became impatient, so they carried the maimed bodies down Barbour Street, which ran alongside the north edge of the lot to an old Italian woman's house. She had a reputation for making fennel tea that cured colic, and parsley paste that halted balding, and garlic mash for stomach ulcer. She placed sliced raw potatoes all over Margie Potter's melted back.

The child was only six months old on the day of the circus fire, and her little overalls were a homespun cotton that protected her legs, but the back of her shirt had caught fire. One of the many doctors who came to treat her in the proceeding years said to his nurse as the two worked above the little girl, sitting before them in her underpants, "I'm going to have to do some research. But I suspect raw potatoes only served to cool the skin, which was, I guess, better than doing nothing." Then, continuing to ponder, he said, "I wonder if a raw potato is a sterile medium . . . if the juice got rid of the bacteria on the woman's hands . . . " Margie blocked out his words at that point and thought about the people who had carried her down Barbour Street. She imagined them saying those words, "Anything is better than doing nothing." Then she blocked out the image, too, and went back to the story-book in her lap. The story of Bambi.

Since Margie's scars were only on her back, she had been able to ignore them pretty much. In fact, she never had any qualms about wearing bathing suits or even strapless gowns, because what she couldn't see, couldn't hurt her, she'd scoff. She was wearing a bathing suit when she met her husband at the beach when she was seventeen.

In point of fact, she'd made his acquaintance the day before when she'd gone out on a fishing boat with her cousin, Little Pete, and his friends, and her two girlfriends. She was the kind of teenager who always went out in groups. Boys were friends, not romantic interests. That was because she was "the girl with the scars,'" which put her off-limits for romance. She did evoke kindness in boys because they all knew about her being in the fire, but when she wore a sleeveless blouse in warm weather, the recoil was there. All the same, the intimacy of group friendships offered her the kind of freedom she appreciated, saving her from having to act adorable, or dumb; and she didn't have to let the boy win when they all went bowling. She found that she did fall into such a pattern when new members joined the group, when she was covered up. But she hated herself when she was act-ing coy. She found herself thinking, what am I doing?

On the fishing boat there were six guys from the next beach who had rented a cottage for a week to celebrate the coming wedding of one of their gang. An extended bachelor party. They were a little older than Margie and her cousin and friends. A bunch of Hartford cops, someone said. She and her girlfriends flirted with them. They flirted back. Margie had on a windbreaker because it was chilly out on the sound. If it hadn't been chilly, she wouldn't have had it on, and they wouldn't have flirted back at her. But then, with her scars showing, she wouldn't have flirted in the first place.

The one getting married was Charlie O'Neill. He seemed

to her to be uneasy about the attention he was getting. His friends kept saying things to him, like, "Your fishing days are about over, old buddy." She caught his eye and smiled. He shrugged. He was embarrassed. He fit in with his group in a lot of ways—same age, same clothes—but was somehow removed. He's uncomfortable, Margie thought. Just the way she was when people tried to act as if she didn't have the scars.

When the captain gave the call to reel in, Charlie was watching her. He came by and said, "Hard to catch anything with no bait."

She said, "Yeah. I like to watch, not fish. I mean, I don't like to watch people fishing, either. I mean . . . I love it out here."

He said, "Yeah," too.

The next day, she was sitting on a blanket on the beach facing into the sun reading a book, *To Kill a Mockingbird*. She was reading it for the second time. Margie had read it in school a few months earlier, and she couldn't bear to leave it, so it was the first in her stack of summer books. Her friends were back at their cottages, sleeping late. She spotted the guys from the boat walking along the beach looking at girls. Charlie O'Neill was about ten feet from her blanket when he noticed her and squinted. He came closer, and he didn't look away when he noticed the trails of scar tissue reaching up and across her shoulders. Not only did he not look away, he actually stared, and then he came right over to her blanket, squatted down, and said, "Where'd you get that?"

He was right level with her. His long eyelashes fluttered. He was pretty nondescript looking, but he had long, dark eyelashes. She said, "The library."

He was confused for just an instant. Then he smiled a tiny bit, and he said, "No. The burns."

She said, "The circus fire."

He said, "Yeah."

Since the circus fire had become an integral component of the city of Hartford's character, there really wasn't much more for him to say than "Yeah." If he'd just come from California, he might have said, "What circus fire?" But there wasn't anyone from California who went to Chalker Beach in Old Saybrook, Connecticut, in 1961.

He said, "Your name's Margie, right?" The eyelashes drew her in.

"How'd you know that?"

"I heard your friends on the boat."

They talked. Charlie and his friends were not cops, they were firemen. Charlie was just a little kid the day the Barnum & Bailey tent went up like a marshmallow on a stick, the ashes blown away by the hot summer breeze until there was nothing left where the tent had been except the twisted animal chute and the stack of black lumps piled up against it. He apologized to Margie for his forward attitude by explaining that it must have been a really formative year for him when the circus burned because he could remember how no one could speak of anything else, day in and day out. He said that's why he'd become a fireman. When everyone else finally stopped talking about the fire, he couldn't stop thinking about it.

Charlie had become obsessed by the Hartford circus fire and was still obsessed now, even though it had happened more than fifteen years before. That was why he was such a dedicated fireman. And when he saw Margie Potter that day at the beach, he became obsessed with her, too. Obsession was a mere romantic notion in those days, not the form of psychopathy it's seen as today. There was a wonderful book then, *Magnificent Obsession*, which was made into a movie with Jane Wyman. To be the object of all the love and desire one man could muster Margie found rather appealing. Romantic. More than romantic. Erotic.

Margie smirked at Charlie. Charlie found that the smirk in

combination with Margie's clear, gray eyes was irresistible. As irresistible as the scars. There was that problem, though, his being engaged. The day Charlie saw Margie on the beach he was two weeks away from getting married. Because of that, he and Margie tried to act as though the connection happening between them as they sat on her blanket wasn't really happening. He asked her about her book, for example. He told her he wasn't a good reader. So Margie relayed to him the whole plot of *To Kill a Mockingbird.* He lay back on his elbows and listened. She read him the scenes with Boo Radley aloud. When she finished, she said, "You may not be a good reader, but you sure are a good listener." He was one of those people whose expression changed in reflection of what someone was telling him. Margie found it endearing rather than comical. She said, "Were you read to a lot when you were little?" And then his expression became blank. The kind of blank when you anticipate something big is going to happen. Margie said, "Hey. What'd I say?"

He relaxed again. "Nothing. No, I was never read to."

She said, "Me neither. But my father used to tell me bedtime stories."

"Like Goldilocks?"

"Nope. Like 'The Fox and the Grapes.' "

He didn't say anything so she told him it was a fable, an Aesop fable. He said, "Oh." She didn't know what to say next, so she said, "Want me to tell it to you?" Then he laughed at her in a quiet way. She laughed at herself, too, in the same silent way.

Charlie said, "Let's swim out to the raft. You can tell it to me out there."

Margie said, "Okay." She got up and pulled on a T-shirt. He watched her. Great body, but so damaged. She said, "Scar tissue gets sunburned bad." He winced a little, but not a wince of revulsion. A wince of sympathy.

They swam out to the raft and then lay on the warm

boards on their stomachs. Margie stared into the sparkle on
the chop and thanked Aesop for fixing her up with Charlie
and at the same time cursed the Lord because Charlie was
engaged. They spent all day together, taking walks and
swimming and just hanging out till his friends came and got
him. One friend was his brother, who was not a fireman.
Charlie introduced Margie to them.

Then he introduced her burns. He said, "Margie got
burned at the circus." All serious, they treated her like a
church relic. Then Charlie said, "See you around, Margie."

She said, "Okay," but while she was saying the word *okay*
and looking into his eyes, she was thinking: I love you.
When she realized she was thinking that, she said to herself,
Oh shit.

They saw each other around that night. They took a walk
to the Indian Town jetty. Indian Town was the next beach,
where Charlie and his friends and brother had rented their
bachelor cottage. They went out to the end of the jetty and
sat down on the rocks a few feet apart. The southern sky was
flaring. Margie said, "What do you suppose that is?"

He said, "Looks like an electrical storm over Long Island."

"It's really beautiful."

He said, "It is. Unless it hits a tree with a few people hiding under it."

Margie thought: Here I am, one of those famous circus
fire victims, and I'm in love with someone who sees lightning and thinks immediately about people getting hit by it.

Then they didn't say anything because she was thinking
about that and thinking about the fact that Charlie was getting married. She figured he was thinking the same thing.
She was right. He said, "I'm getting married to get my mind
off all this."

"All this?"

"The circus fire."

"Oh."

"I'm driving my family crazy."

"Because you aren't married?"

"Sort of. Because I don't care about marriage. All I care about is figuring out who set it."

"Who set what?"

He paused. "Margie, the fire. But I'm getting discouraged. And my mother kept threatening to call the old country and have a bride sent from L'Aquila."

"Where?"

"A town in Italy. Where my grandparents came from."

"I thought you said your name was O'Neill."

"My mother's name was DeNardo."

"Oh." Then Margie, looking over to him, said, "The circus fire was an accident."

Charlie's gaze didn't shift from the horizon. "No, it wasn't."

She said, "How come I don't know that?"

He looked at her with his long eyelashes. Italian eyelashes. "You're too young."

"So tell me about it."

"I don't want to make you feel bad."

"I was just a baby, Charlie. It's never really meant anything to me."

Then he scooted over next to her, put his arm around her shoulders, across the bumps and ridges, and he told her.

Charlie said to Margie that all the firemen knew it had been set, but firemen have lots of other fires to worry about—the ones that they have to fight every single day. Their job was to put them out, not concern themselves with how they started. In those days, fire marshalls didn't have any clout; the police were supposed to figure out who, if anyone, set suspicious fires, and the police in 1944 had concluded that the fire had been an accident, though a catastrophic one. But that was because the chief of police had accepted fifty free tickets to the circus in lieu of an inspection. Back then, bribery wasn't considered psychopathic any more than obsession was. So out of guilt, the Hartford Police Department had announced within one week of the rack and ruin, with so many people dead and injured, that the fire had been an accident. They had planned to say it was an accident even while it was happening, was what Charlie told Margie. They went by the theory that the tent had been lit by a flipped cigarette butt.

Then he changed the subject. Margie had been somehow cuddling up closer to him. He became sheepish and told Margie that, besides all the discouragement, Sylvia was a very beautiful girl.

Charlie could see Margie's chest rise. She asked, "That's your fiancée? Sylvia?"

"Yeah."

Margie let out the big breath she'd taken.

Chapter Two

When Margie met Charlie it was right after her high school graduation, during the last week of June. She'd given herself a two-week vacation before she would have to start her job as a clerk in the Records Department at the Travelers. She would be working at the Travelers even though she was college material.

Not many students in the Hartford High graduating class of '61 were college material, but Margie got very high grades, and so was lumped together with that group of luminaries with whom she had nothing in common but report cards. Margie had dreaded her junior-year counseling appointment when she'd have to go head-to-head with Miss Foss, the girls' guidance counselor. Miss Foss was tall and had the same face as the wicked stepmother in Walt Disney's *Snow White,* except that she didn't have the skin-tight black snood instead of hair. Miss Foss's hair was snoodlike, though, pulled back sleekly into a perfectly round bun. Her bun looked like a baseball made of anthracite. No gentle and carefree tendrils for Miss Foss. Margie admired her absolute absence of vanity. And Miss Foss admired Margie's joy of books and was intrigued by her general persona, as well, since Margie's background didn't match Miss Foss's image of a voracious reader. At the appointment, Margie told her she didn't know what she wanted to do after high school, but she did know that she wasn't interested in attending college.

Miss Foss said to her, "But you understand *Mah*-jorie, that you are college material."

Margie's real name wasn't Marjorie, it was Martha, but she ignored the error since she was so used to people making it. Also, there wasn't any point in correcting the woman, since Margie wouldn't ever speak with her again. In those days, a high school student spoke with her counselor once. So Margie just said, "Yeah."

Miss Foss still felt free to correct Margie, even though she knew, too, that she'd never lay eyes on the girl again. She said, "*Yes, Mah*-jorie. *Yeah* is a cheap word now, isn't it?" Her tone when she repeated the word *yeah* was the same as if she were given no choice but to utter something foul, Margie thought, like *boilsucker*.

Margie said, "Yes, Miss Foss, it is. Sorry."

Miss Foss was leaning on her forearms, hands together, fingers laced, staring intently into Margie's eyes. "Do you intend to remain ignorant of the possibilities of which a girl of your talent and intelligence might take advantage?"

Margie said, "Only my grades are college material, Miss Foss. But not me."

Miss Foss's gaze remained intent. "That is a point well taken. Intelligence does not necessarily result in ambition. To be ambitious is to be willing to take risks. One such risk is abandoning one's . . . one's background." Her nostrils narrowed just before the word *background*.

"I don't want to abandon my background, Miss Foss. I like my background."

The hands disengaged. Miss Foss leaned back in her office chair, which was not Hartford High issue. It was her own, upholstered, and it supported the small of her back. Miss Foss slouching was beyond anyone's imagination. She said to Margie, "I am blunt with all my *gulls, Mah*-jorie. I am afraid I am compelled to tell you that I see you as the proverbial worm in the jar of horseradish."

Margie hadn't ever heard or read of that proverb. And there were no bumper stickers or message T-shirts then. "I'm sorry?"

Miss Foss smiled. She appreciated Margie's subtle sarcasm. "You find living in horseradish acceptable, lovely, even . . . " and now she leaned forward again, forearms back on the desk, hands clasped, " . . . because you've never been out of the jar."

Miss Foss had never tasted horseradish, Margie thought. Miss Foss had never been out of her jar of tea and crumpets. Margie didn't say any of that, though, because she was taught by her father to be respectful. Then Miss Foss retreated and proceeded instead to let her curiosity get the best of her. She said, "I understand you are the youngest casualty of the circus fire. "

Margie had never thought of it like that, never knew she possessed a unique notoriety. The youngest. Because she was thinking, she didn't respond, and so Miss Foss filled in the growing gap.

"And that your mother was killed."

Now Margie looked straight into Miss Foss's eyes. "Yes."

Miss Foss raised her two forefingers and made a steeple. Against her better judgment, knowing that the entire line of the day's appointments would now be three minutes behind schedule, she continued, "You do not, as yet, understand your burden. But on some level you know that any risks you might take will bring you closer to facing that burden. I wish, Mah-jorie, that you would—"

Margie said, "Leave me alone." Margie could be forceful when respect didn't work. She stood up. Miss Foss said nothing, just continued to gaze at her as she went to the door.

Then the woman said, "I believe in you, *Mah*-jorie," but Margie didn't turn back. Miss Foss was lying. Margie was thinking, I'm just a curiosity to her.

Miss Foss couldn't know that whether she tossed Margie some crumb or whether she didn't, nothing would have changed the girl's mind. The definitive moment—the one that told Margie what she should do when high school ended—had come to her one morning on the city bus as it traveled down Broad Street toward Hartford High. Margie's mind had been somewhere in that spacey place between waking up and the Pledge of Allegiance. But there had been a distraction this day. Two girls who were last year's graduates had taken the bus to work because of car problems. They worked at the Travelers in downtown Hartford. They wore pastel-colored spring suits. Their hair was done up in professional beehives. They had on pale high heels to match their suits. They didn't carry lunch bags. They would eat at a downtown café. They both had fresh diamonds on their left hands. The two had stood in the aisle of the bus gripping the chrome poles, chatting merrily. Wide awake. The polish of their fingernails and the glitter of their diamonds gripped Margie. The girls were grown up. And that was what she wanted to be. Grown up. Margie didn't like being a kid. College meant staying a kid for another four years, being dependent on her father, who lived for a precise kind of freedom he would avail himself of only when Margie became self-sufficient. Margie sensed that about her father, but besides, she never really enjoyed being a student, which meant being a kid. Which meant making her father wait.

It would have surprised Miss Foss to know that Margie hated studying. She loved to read, and she tended to remember what she'd read, but Margie knew that was not studying, it was good fortune. Now she wanted a job where she could meet a husband. Then she could stay at home with the babies that would come and she would be able to read, untroubled. So, as if the Blue Fairy had intended to grant her wish but happened to be in a bit of a hurry, she flew in, made a quick pass with her magic wand, and Charlie appeared before Margie even began the job that was supposed to serve as a husband hunt. Of course, within seconds of meeting her, Charlie wanted to kill himself because of his poor timing. But Margie told him later that if he hadn't been engaged, he wouldn't have been living it up at his bachelor cottage just down the road from her Uncle Pete and Aunt Jane's summer cottage and they'd never have met. It was fortuitous; they were star-crossed, Margie assured him. When she told him that, he knew what she meant by star-crossed, but Margie could tell he'd never heard the word *fortuitous*.

Afterward, he used the word in the correct context so Margie realized he'd gone and looked it up. His thoughtfulness filled her with affection, which helped her get by the hysterical phone calls that soon arrived from Sylvia, and the guilt she felt for not feeling guilty. She did feel guilty about her role in Charlie's betrayal of Sylvia; what she didn't feel guilty about was having sex the week she met him.

It didn't hurt at all to lose her virginity. Maybe if it had, she would have felt God's punishment. She didn't bleed, either. Margie figured pain and bleeding must have been just another couple of lies to keep girls from wanting to make love to someone when it felt natural to do. Charlie's eyes were locked into hers when Margie lost her virginity and his eyes were stricken. Margie stopped anticipating pain because she thought Charlie was in pain. Afterwards, the first thing he said was, "I'm sorry." Then he said, "I love you."

Margie smiled in empathy. Then she said, "I want to do that again," so that he'd know nothing hurt. Also because she really did want to do it again.

He blinked little tears. Margie was overcome with love and kindly feeling toward him. She covered his face with kisses. She kissed him and kissed him and so they did do it again. Margie couldn't believe how easy it was to love someone. And the love Charlie felt from her gave him such a grand relief that while she lay in his arms after the second time, he was able to ask her what he'd wanted to ask her ever since he saw her reading on the beach. He asked, "Margie. What happened to you?"

She wondered if he was asking her if she experienced orgasm so she said, "Nothing. But I bet it will happen next time." His expression told her she'd misinterpreted the question so she explained what she'd thought he meant. He just stared at her for the longest time, and he said, "Oh, God." Then he said, "Next time, I promise you. If it takes all day." Margie started to ask him what that meant—if *what* took all day?—but he was already explaining what he'd meant in the first place. "What I want to know is, what happened to you the day of the fire?"

"Oh." So Margie told him that she really didn't know what happened to her. She was, after all, the youngest casualty. A baby. She said, "I can only tell you what other people told me." And he said, "Please tell me what they told you."

So she told him in bits and pieces, starting with the bucket brigade and the lady with the potatoes. He said, "Emilia Pasqucci."

He knew the Italian woman's name. He said that was because his mother had been born and brought up in the once Italian stronghold at the north end of the city. Everyone there knew everyone else. That was a half-truth. He knew the name of Emilia Pasqucci not because of his mother, who undoubtedly did know the woman, but because of his obsession. He knew every single fact, every name, every particular connected with the circus fire. Margie would come to find that out soon.

While they talked, Margie could see how happy he was to have found her—how happy not to have to relinquish his obsession, even though there was this huge complication he'd have to face, relinquishing the beautiful Sylvia and calling off his wedding. Margie went on with her story, still in bits and pieces because they kept breaking up the narrative with passionate kissing. They were making love down by the creek at the end of the beach where there was privacy. Mosquitoes were why no one went to the creek. Margie and Charlie never felt the mosquitoes feasting on them. All that week, Charlie kept running out of condoms and finally thought to buy a bottle of insect repellent during his many trips to the drugstore.

After they finally reached the point where they could control themselves somewhat, Margie was able just to sit placidly in Charlie's arms and tell him her story without interruptions. She did it the same way she had described the plot of *To Kill a Mockingbird*, the way she described any good book she recommended to a friend. Dramatically. In fact, she blurted out the words, "My mother died in the fire trying to save me," knowing Charlie would take them very hard. In fact, his eyes became big love-crumbs, Margie thought, as e.e. cummings put it so sublimely. Charlie said, "Your mother died? In the fire?"

"Yes."

He was completely overcome, his face filled with dreadful grief. She went on, telling Charlie that the surge of the thousands of hysterical people must have wrenched her from her mother's arms. She told him that even though almost all of the dead were crushed up against the animal chute, her mother wasn't because she wasn't trying to get out; she was trying to find her baby.

Charlie swallowed. She watched his Adam's apple go up and down. "And your father?" he asked.

"He was overseas. Actually, he was in a prisoner-of-war camp. He didn't find out my mother had died till he was liberated."

"Jesus." Charlie hugged her closer. "Where did they find her?"

"Under the grandstand. Under the Grandstand C seats is what I heard. What was left of the Grandstand C seats."

Charlie crushed her to him and kissed her. He said, "Someone—whoever it was—saved you. Saved you for me. God bless him."

Margie thought, Yeah. She decided it wasn't the moment to mention that the blessed person left his thumbprint in her back. Then Charlie pulled off Margie's bathing suit and made love to her again. What he'd promised her earlier didn't take all day.

When Margie emerged from the magical tunnel Charlie created that led to her having an orgasm, she lay in his arms thinking how interesting it was that the one thing Charlie didn't say, which everyone else said to her when they asked her about the fire, was, "Well, at least the animal act was over. A merciful thing." Margie couldn't believe how morbid people were. As if the fire alone hadn't been bad enough, people liked to imagine the big cats eating people as the flames burned all around. Charlie obviously understood that things were morbid enough without such black flights of fancy.

But Charlie did know it was a merciful thing, not because the animals would have eaten anyone—they were very well fed—but because the circus was not just any circus, it was the Ringling Brothers and Barnum & Bailey's, the Greatest Show on Earth, and in those days, the wild animal act was not a tame Siberian tiger and a few tired-looking lions. The Ringlings had the best. The Alfred Court Wild Animal Act had forty lions, thirty tigers, thirty leopards, twenty bears, and forty elephants. It was some show.

The line, "The animals had just cleared the chute," came

up over and over in stories about the circus fire. No one could quite visualize the animals clearing the chute, even people who had been to the circus several times, but Charlie could. He'd studied the catastrophe from beginning to end. He knew that the reason the people couldn't picture the scene was because it happened so swiftly. The illusion was that it didn't happen at all. At the Hartford circus, the chute ran from the enormous cage in the ring nearest the main entrance and on out of a slit in the tent a few feet from the main entrance where it met up with the circus-train cages. The chute was an arch of metal bars. As soon as the animal act ended, the lights would go out and a spot would come on, aimed at the saddest of all sad clowns, Emmett Kelly, who would wring such poignant feelings out of the hearts of the crowd that all eyes would remain riveted on him. And then, after his act of diversion, he'd slip out of the spot and the beam of light would swing up to the peak of the tent. And there, as if by a miracle, perched on a tiny wood platform, were the Flying Wallendas about to walk the tightrope. In the moment before the first Wallenda stepped out onto the rope, the circus hands would have already dismantled the cage and chute. But not on the day of the fire.

Emmett Kelly had missed his cue. The Ringmaster counted to three, and when the clown still hadn't appeared, signaled for the spot to go out. So the audience, that afternoon, watched the animals trot through the chute, the roustabouts take down the cage, and the Wallendas climb their ladder. The roustabouts were just turning their attention to the chute when they saw the beginnings of the fire. The men scrambled off to safety, leaving the chute where it stood. Consequently, anyone who tried to get to the main entrance from Grandstand A in the southwest corner of the tent had to climb over the chute in order to escape. Hundreds of people did try, but only the Wallendas were able to do it, and, of course, do it with ease, as they were acrobats.

But Margie's mother was found under the ashes of the wooden seats in Grandstand C. She had died of smoke inhalation while she searched, was what Margie's father told her and what she told Charlie. People would say to her father—nasty, stupid people—why would anyone take an infant to a circus? Her father would tell them in his beaten voice, "The baby was her closest friend." He never got over the ridiculous irony that he survived a prisoner-of-war camp while his wife couldn't make it through a circus.

When Margie told Charlie about the nasty, stupid people, he said, "Stop, stop," and hugged her and petted her and told her he adored her. His face reflected the pain she insisted she didn't feel. It was just a story. "Charlie, I have no memory of any of this!"

During their conspiratorial meetings at the creek, it finally came to be Margie's turn to ask Charlie what happened to him at the circus. What with the obsession, she'd assumed he'd been there. He told her he hadn't been, but that he'd had a ticket. She smiled, of course, and then he smiled, too. The circus fire had become such a legend in Hartford that anyone in the city who wasn't at the circus claimed they'd had a ticket but were saved because they missed the last bus, or because they chose not to go as it was just too hot that day, or whatever. As if people throw away a ticket to the circus because it's hot.

Charlie asked, "So what'd you get?"

He meant her settlement. They hadn't had class-action suits back then. They hardly had any lawsuits at all. But the Ringlings wanted to do right by the victims. They paid the families, and the injured survivors, an amount deemed appropriate by a volunteer panel of Connecticut probate judges who determined each casualty's level of loss or injury. They awarded a cash amount to the next of kin of the dead and more complicated settlements to the physically injured. Uninjured survivors didn't expect to be recompensed for their emotional trauma—that you escaped the fire untouched was recompense enough. To complain about the damage to your psyche was to trivialize those who were really hurt. There wasn't such a thing as post-traumatic stress syndrome till Vietnam. Margie's father's condition would, today, have been considered post-traumatic stress. In World War II, people who had nervous breakdowns were pretty much thought of as cowards.

Not only did the judges consider the condition of each claimant, they also took into account the age of the claimant. Margie's settlement would be a new Cadillac every year for the rest of her life, to be received on her birthday rather than on the anniversary of the fire, which was initially suggested before the judges suddenly looked at one another, chagrined. One of them said, "We're going off the deep end, here, fellas." The youngest victims all got cars. That way, the judges felt, the children's guardians wouldn't be able to abscond with large lump sums of money. The Ringlings made deals with several automobile companies. Margie's getting Cadillacs instead of Fords was the luck of the draw.

As Margie grew up, and came to understand all that had happened, her executor, her father, told her she could have the cars once she graduated from high school and got a job. So at the beach, in the summer of '61, she was driving her first one, dazzling the boys with a pink-and-black Eldorado convertible. But Charlie was dazzled by her scars.

When he made love to her in her bed at Aunt Jane's one night when her aunt and uncle had gone to the movies, Charlie felt the thumbprint.

She was lying on top of him, looking down into his eyes while his fingers were tracing the ridges of scars on her back.

Then he felt the oval thumbprint in the small of her back, and stopped what he was doing even though he was inside her. His erection went away and he slid out from under her, kept her on her stomach under the lamplight, and from behind her he said, "Margie, you've got a fingerprint down here."

Margie said, "Thumbprint."

He rolled her over. She felt embarrassed lying on her back, naked in the light because her breasts fell into her armpits, not like the centerfolds in *Playboy*—theirs stayed straight up, pointed.

Charlie got all concerned. He said, "Margie, I'm sorry! Please don't be ashamed."

So she told him the thumbprint scar wasn't the problem. She told him she was embarrassed by suddenly being flat-chested and made reference to the magazine. He rolled his eyes. He said, "Silly girl. Centerfold breasts are taped to stay upright and then the tape gets airbrushed out." Firemen had determined that because they were surrounded by centerfolds adorning their walls. Back then, at least. So he kissed her flat chest where her breasts would have come together if she was standing, and he said, "This is a nice place when you're on your back, Margie. I get closer to your heart." Then he laid his head on the middle of her chest, listening to her heart-beat, and said, "Lub-dub, lub-dub, lub-dub." Then, trusting that it wouldn't take any more effort to get Margie by that bit of insecurity, he asked, "Whose thumbprint is it?"

Margie said, "Everyone's told me it was probably one of the soldiers," and she described the people-brigade, which was nothing new to him.

"I've met some of those fellas," he said. "Jesus Christ, Margie."

Margie said, "Could you get back inside me?"

Charlie said, "I'd better get on the phone is where I'd better get. I've decided I'm not going to wait till I get home to tell Sylvia. She doesn't deserve this."

Yeah, Margie thought. It was true. She didn't.

Chapter Three

Margie and Charlie went out on the fishing boat again on Charlie's last day at the beach. Usually, in the summer, the horizon was obscured by a humid haze, but now the air had been dried out by a Canadian front. Margie said, "When it's this clear, Long Island seems so close that I feel like I could swim there in ten minutes."

Charlie said, "The guys cornered me last night."

"They did?"

"Yeah. They wanted to know what the hell was going on." So did Margie. "What did you tell them?"

"I told them that Sylvia and I had broken up."

"Then what happened?"

"They just sat around wondering what they should say, but then my brother Michael—he's kind of a comedian—he said, 'Is it too late to change the cake?'"

"What cake?"

"The cake that says 'Charlie and Sylvia' on it. For the party. Half the department's coming down from Hartford tonight."

"Oh." She waited, but he didn't say any more. "Charlie?"

"Yeah?"

"What did Sylvia say?"

He leaned back into the wood bench, put his head back, and looked up at the drifting clouds. "She just started crying. She tried to say something but she was crying too hard to talk. Then her father got on the phone so I told him, too."

"Pretty hard, I guess."

"Not really. I mean, well, it was. He kept saying, 'These things happen.' But then he started crying, too."

"I'm sorry, Charlie."

"I know."

He hugged Margie to him. She put her hand under his shirt and rubbed his chest. "What about the cake?"

"Well, Michael has this kind of protective attitude toward me so he said to the guys, 'When the cake comes, just scrape off *Sylvia* and write in *Margie.*'"

"Making a joke of things isn't especially protective, I don't think."

"I guess that isn't what I meant, then. He tried to get our minds off it."

Margie would not make a joke to ease Charlie's responsibilities. But, like his brother, she would divert him. It seemed like a good time to satisfy her own curiosity.

"Charlie?"

"What, honey?"

"Why do you not believe that maybe—just maybe—a lit cigarette butt started the fire?"

"Margie, the cigarette theory is bullshit."

Then he took his arm down from around her shoulders, touched her chin, and she turned her face to his. He tried to tell *her* a story. She watched his expression change from deliberation, to frustration, to sadness. A great story was going on in his head. She said, "Go ahead, Charlie, tell me."

He said, "Someone tried to murder you. Murder you and all those other people who went to the circus just to have fun."

She began to protest, but his finger slid up from her chin to her lips.

"See, it wasn't just the worst *fire* in Connecticut's history. It was the worst *crime* in Connecticut's history. A hundred and sixty-nine people murdered. Over a thousand maimed."

Maimed? That was Margie he was talking about. She said, "I don't feel maimed."

When she said that, Charlie grabbed her into his arms and hugged her so tightly she thought he'd break her ribs. But she let him hug. Once he'd calmed, Charlie gave her more details, just like all of Aesop's details in "The Fox and the Grapes." He told her he'd spoken to a few firemen who had been involved with the Hartford circus fire. One of them had been a rookie at the time and for some reason had gotten in on the experiment. They'd set up a sawhorse on a day that had the same weather conditions as the day of the circus. They had coated a piece of canvas with the paraffin-and-gasoline mix and had thrown the canvas over the sawhorse. They couldn't get it to light until they used matches, and not only did they need matches, they had to hold a match to the canvas for a good while before it caught. And the flame needed a tiny breeze to get it going, too, the same tiny breeze there had been on the day of the fire. The firemen said they all had to blow on it. Inside the circus tent, the air had been stagnant. Charlie said, "No way that tent would have caught from a flipped cigarette. Not from inside the tent. The guilty party here wasn't a careless person flipping a lit butt, Margie. It was an arson-ist."

And Margie imagined a cruel and evil man whistling far and wee, with a name like Uriah Heep, slinking along the tent, finding a quiet spot to torch it, while inside, the children laughed. She said, "I don't want to believe that."

"Of course you don't. No one wanted to believe it, and they still don't."

"Why not? If it's the truth."

Charlie thought for a minute. He tried to explain. "If the Ringlings went ahead and proved it was arson, people might think twice about going to the circus. People love the circus because there's danger, but the danger isn't to them; they just get to watch it. A fire, that's another story. So the circus guys said, 'Yes, isn't this awful? We're so sorry.' They proved to everyone how sorry they were by going off to jail. They were negligent so they would take their punishment."

"Who exactly went to jail?" Margie had visions of clowns and aerialists being carted off to jail in costume.

"The four officers of the circus. Connecticut never needed to file extradition papers. The men didn't appeal the decision. They went to jail for six months. Not because they wanted to—I mean they weren't jerks—they did it to save the circus."

Margie said, "The power of positive thinking." That was an actual title of a book by Dr. Norman Vincent Peale that everyone was reading. Not Margie. She didn't like real books.

"Yeah. Exactly. The war was going on. Full steam. That was enough to take in. Forget about nutcases going around burning down a circus in the middle of the matinee per-formance."

Margie asked, "So where is he?"

"Who?"

"The arsonist?"

Charlie gazed out across the lovely sound, at the bumps of Long Island. "Out there."

The second member of Charlie's family Margie met, after his brother Michael, was his Uncle Chick, who drove down to Old Saybrook when Michael called him. Charlie was his namesake. His godfather. Margie had heard of Chick DeNardo. A lot of people had. He'd been a detective with the Hartford Police Department; he'd just retired. Every year on the anniversary of the circus fire, Chick and his old partner from 1944 would place a nosegay of forget-me-nots on the grave of Little Miss 1565, an unidentified victim of the fire— a child who had been the 1,565th casualty to arrive at the Hartford Hospital catastrophe triage. Every year, photographs of Chick and his partner laying the nosegay on the granite marker would flash around the world via the AP.

The doctors guessed Little Miss 1565 to be around seven years old. She had lived just long enough for a nurse at the hospital to start an IV. Then the nurse noticed that she had died. And nobody claimed her. Day after day, the newspapers called for her family to come forward, but no family did. Were all her relatives lost in the fire? Or was she from an itinerant family who couldn't afford to bury her and just left town in their grief?

Or was she left behind, deliberately, hopefully, alive, her down-and-out family knowing that the grieving community would be able to take better care of her than they? There were lots of guesses, but in the end, no conclusions.

In the attempt to identify her, the police decided to take a photo of her—her face had been left practically untouched by the flames. Her left cheek was blackened, and so the camera was positioned to her right. The nurses washed the soot from her and combed her beautiful blond curls into a soft halo, each curl delicately laid out against a white pillow under her head. She had long eyelashes that touched softly upon her cheeks. The photo came out looking more like a professional portrait than a police shot. Yes, she looked like a doll, a delicate bisque doll. Yes, a Botticelli angel, as people would say. But she also looked unmistakably dead.

So all across the country, American families came to feel a kinship toward the Little Miss because of that extraordinarily beautiful photo taken at Hartford Hospital just before she was taken away to be buried in a grave donated by a local cemetery. Later, the grave was marked by a block of granite that read: LITTLE MISS 1565—GONE BUT NOT FORGOTTEN.

The unidentified child hadn't died of her burns, and she hadn't suffocated, either, as Margie Potter's mother had. She had died of compression injuries, the way almost all of the victims had died, crushed up against the bars of the wild animal chute: hairline skull fractures, internal abdominal trauma, broken ribs puncturing her lungs. She had been pulled, still alive, from the very bottom of the pile of bodies.

Margie had wondered if her own saviors, who had handed her to Hermes Wallenda, had been standing on Little Miss 1565. She never wondered that aloud until she met Charlie, and he said, "Probably," without skipping a beat. He meant yes.

Chick was obsessed with who that little girl was, just as Charlie was obsessed with who set the fire. "Yeah," Charlie would say, "we're both obsessed. My uncle is obsessed with who she is and I'm obsessed with who killed her." *Killed her* brought Uriah Heep back again into Margie's mind. At the time of the fire, Chick's own two little girls—Charlie's cousins—had been around the age of the Little Miss, so

Chick had been beside himself with wanting to know how people could have lost such a lovely child and not claimed her. Chick always felt that if there had been an arsonist, he'd have been killed by the fire too, just like Little Miss 1565. It was Chick's Italian roots that convinced him that justice must have been rendered. That belief allowed him to carry out his particular sad search instead of the search his nephew was to take up years later.

Charlie kept on explaining things to Margie. None of the policemen believed that the fire was an accident, either, he said, even though the chief said it was. However, what they did believe was that the arsonist had miscalculated, never imagining the holocaust that would erupt because of the lethal makeup of the tent. And so he must have died, too, like Chick said, unable to escape the hell he'd ignited.

At first, Chick tried to convince Charlie of this theory, but Charlie couldn't be convinced. He said to Margie, "Arsonists are never careless. They aren't suicidal, either. He set the fire, deliberately, outside the tent, behind Grandstand A."

Margie said, "But the fire started ten feet off the ground."

Charlie said, "More like twelve. And you're forgetting the wind."

Margie didn't say it to Charlie, or to Chick, or to anyone else that she really didn't believe someone set the fire. The cigarette theory made perfect sense to her. She figured, maybe when the firemen tried to re-create the start of the fire, they didn't actually flip a cigarette into a piece of canvas. Maybe the force of the actual flip caused the butt to lodge into the side of the tent, into the sticky paraffin. She was so sure that no one would deliberately do such a thing as terrible as setting fire to a circus tent full of people that she felt free to humor Charlie.

In fact, she couldn't resist. His obsession was irresistible to her. It was like living an adventure book, a grand novel of suspense, a spy thriller, a detective mystery, a perfect crime. And besides that, if Charlie was right and there was an arsonist after all, and if Charlie found him, that arsonist would have hell to pay. She could sense Charlie's anger just sitting and waiting for its chance. What he might be capable of gave her tingles.

Finally, when all that could be said about the fire had been said, and Margie and Charlie were back in Hartford, they met and talked, instead, about what all new lovers talk about—themselves. Actually, Margie did most of the talking. Charlie wanted every single tiny detail of her—of all that she was. It took hours just getting by Charter Oak Terrace.

"You lived in Charter Oak Terrace? You *lived* there?" It was more a shocked response than a question.

The Hartford Fire Department spent a lot of time in Charter Oak Terrace. Today you hear about low-cost housing projects—projects, in the plural. But for a long time Charter Oak Terrace, named for the famous tree where the patriots hid the country's first document claiming independence, was the only low-income housing project in Hartford, the first one in Connecticut, and it came to be known as "the Project," singular. When Margie was a child, she didn't tell people she lived in the Project. Instead, she'd say, "I live in Charter Oak Terrace." The name was very spirited to her, and beautiful, too. Magnificent tales of revolutionary heroes lived in those words. But then people would look at her sadly, or disdainfully, and say, "Oh. The Project."

Charter Oak Terrace had been a forty-acre tract of land on either side of a small polluted river, a branch of the main river flowing through Hartford called the Hog, which is a branch of the Connecticut River. Nowadays, the

Hog River flows through pipes, underground, under Interstate 84, and Margie thought it was buried because of its name. Charter Oak Terrace, however, was as pastoral as its lovely name, and the branch of the Hog was cleaned up for the opening of the Project. She recalled fondly the stream as being quite clear with little pools to catch sunnies in. Even though there was row after row of two-story, cinder-block buildings, they were laid out in wide grids with plenty of green grass to play on between, and with oak trees everywhere, planted in honor of the famous one. The narrow roads within the Project were only traveled by the cars of people who lived there, and there weren't many of those because in those days, people took the city buses everywhere and didn't need cars. If you were poor, like the women living in the Project whose husbands had gone off to war, you couldn't afford a car anyway.

A little school, kindergarten through second grade, was built for the Project children. Once the kids hit third grade, the planners figured they were old enough to walk the mile and a half to the nearest full-fledged elementary school. The little Charter Oak Terrace school had a wonderful playground that the children could use whenever they wanted, not just during school hours. One day when Margie was five, she'd bet her friend that she could pump her swing so hard that she would go all the way up and over the bar and around again. She pumped and pumped till she was perpendicular with the bar, and then the laws of gravity took over. She remembered this so well because of her frustration, and because later, when she got home, she had two huge blisters on the backs of her knees. Her Aunt Jane got all teary-eyed. Margie's blisters recalled burns. Aunt Jane told her she couldn't swing again till the blisters went away.

When Margie recalled her childhood in Charter Oak

Terrace for Charlie, she described paradise: The ice-cream man in summer; tobogganing down the frozen streets in winter; getting her picture taken in a donkey cart; having to make several runs trick-or-treating because with all those families, the Project kids got lots of treats. There was just one thing missing—a mother. It wasn't unusual not to have a father since they were all overseas, but Margie was motherless, as well, and lived with her Aunt Jane and her cousin, Little Pete, until their fathers came home from the war.

Margie's Aunt Jane had been very close to her mother, and used to say to her—in fact still said to her—"Your mother and I were best buddies." Her mother and her Aunt Jane were married to brothers. Once Margie's father and her Uncle Pete came home from the war, they all stayed on in Charter Oak Terrace for a few years until they got established in new jobs.

Negro people from the South looking for work were moving in after the war, and then when her father and uncle found employment with Fuller Brush, they became disqualified for low-income housing. How Margie hated to go. That was because the Negro people who moved in had more kids than the white families. Margie and Little Pete could just go outside, throw down a hat, call it home plate, and in a minute there were enough kids for two teams.

Now, Charter Oak Terrace was a slum. The black families were replaced by poor Hispanics. Margie and Charlie went to Puerto Rico on their honeymoon and the housing projects in San Juan looked just like Charter Oak Terrace. Except there was no turquoise sea at the end of the narrow streets, only the Hog. And it wasn't a clean little stream anymore, it was a death trap. Latino kids from the Project drowned in the stream made deep with garbage, and junk, and bedsprings, and tires.

After they'd moved, Margie's Aunt Jane learned to drive because she and Uncle Pete moved to a Hartford suburb, and she'd take Little Pete and Margie for a ride to the old neighborhood so they could see where they'd lived before their fathers got back on their feet. The true reason she did this was to check on the weeping cherry tree Margie's mother had planted in front of Aunt Jane's kitchen window as a birthday present. It was always there and it was always bigger. Aunt Jane said to Margie, "Your mother loved beautiful things. She wanted me to see something beautiful while I did the dishes."

After Margie told Charlie that, she buried her head in his chest, and he thought she was crying. But she wasn't. She was willing away crying.

Chapter Four

Margie's formal introduction to the O'Neill clan was at Sunday dinner. Charlie's mother, Palma (she was born on Palm Sunday), held Sunday dinner every week for her brothers and their wives and their kids and her sons, and her sons' wives and kids. Around two dozen people, give or take a couple of newborns, were there to greet Margie. Charlie had warned her about one thing before they arrived; he warned her about her future father-in-law, who would most likely be too hungover to come to the table. Sometimes he was still drunk from Saturday night. Sometimes even still drinking. He was served his dinner in the living room where he'd be parked in front of the TV. If he made it to the dining room, he would sit, eat, and leave. "Best to just ignore him," Charlie told Margie.

Margie had grown up having a father who cooked her

meals and cleaned up until she was old enough to take turns with him. Once, she and her father considered the advantages and disadvantages of helping each other every night, as opposed to alternating shifts, where one would do everything one night, and nothing the next. They decided on the latter so that at least one of them could spend the dinner hour undisturbed, reading. They were both terrible cooks and they both hated to clean dirty dishes, so having one night to do none of those things gave them the fortitude to do it on alternating nights. Margie and her father weren't interested in food. Meals just gave them something to do while they read.

At her first Sunday dinner at Palma's (once the calamitous trauma of Charlie's disengagement from Sylvia and subsequent engagement to her had subsided), Margie was steered toward the kitchen, where all the women were breading veal cutlets, or stirring marinara sauce, or boiling great pots of gnocchi, and, at the same time, getting all the serving dishes, and china, and glasses, and silver organized to set the table. The kitchen was just off the living room. Through the open doorway, Margie watched as the men sat in the living room drinking wine or beer and nibbling on munchies. The patriarch, Denny O'Neill, had an area set off to himself, and to Margie it seemed as if one of those invisible electric fences surrounded him—even the kids knew just how close they could get without risking a shock. Margie was not introduced to him. The point was not to disturb the man so that he wouldn't, in turn, disturb Sunday dinner. So Margie stood in the doorway watching the two scenes: the men talking about the football game they were watching, and the women talking about politics, menopause, religion, books, movies, education, breast cancer, and each other's personal lives.

Then, from upstairs, came the unmistakable sound of kids fighting. Serious fight, Margie could tell, not just a tiff. Mike's wife said to her, "Here, Margie, work on the antipasto while I see what's up." She handed Margie a bunch of radishes and an instrument that would turn them into starbursts. Margie said to her, "Mike isn't doing anything. Can't he break up the fight?" But Mike's wife had already dried her hands and had darted out of the kitchen. So Margie sat down and destroyed the radishes.

Later, when the food was all cooked, the women served the men and children, ate with them, and then cleaned up everything while the men continued to sit and eat pie and drink cups of coffee. The women would grab dessert later, on the run, between getting kids into pajamas and cleaning out or packaging all the debris and leftovers.

In the car, when Charlie drove her home, she told him how shocked she was by the dinner scene. He had no idea why. She told him why. He said, "Well, that's the way my mother wants it."

Margie said, "Lots of slaves thought they liked being slaves." (She didn't say, A lot of worms think horseradish is pheasant under glass.) "I was humiliated for your mother, Charlie."

He said, "It's the way it is."

She said, "I'm going to have to call your mother and explain why I can't come to Sunday dinner anymore. You made it sound like a nice little weekly party, Charlie. But it isn't."

"Jesus, Margie, you'll really hurt my mother's feelings."

"But *my* feelings were hurt."

Charlie, from day one at the beach in Old Saybrook, did what Margie asked. That's because she was not a demanding person; she asked for very little. And Charlie was an insightful person. He understood her feelings once she expressed them. In fact, a year later, when they were at a firemen's picnic, everyone was talking about what a dog Betty Friedan was and Charlie said, "All she wants is a fair shake." That day, Margie had looked over at Charlie and loved him all the more. Everyone else looked down at their hamburgers, confused.

Charlie said to her, "Margie, don't call my mother. Let me do it."

Charlie's compromises always worked with her. But she did ask, "What are you going to tell her?"

"About how you feel. And how I'm going to have to help out next Sunday or you won't come."

He looked over at her from behind the wheel and smirked.

The most erotic thing for a woman is a man who tries to please her, Margie decided. An erotic thing for a man is to watch a woman take off her shoes, unhook her garters, and roll down her stockings, which is what Margie did. He pulled the car into the back of a church parking lot and they climbed over each other into the backseat, kissing and undressing and trying not to suffocate each other.

The next Sunday, Charlie came into the kitchen and started stirring the sauce. At first, everyone laughed and then they all got uncomfortable when they realized it wasn't a joke. The kids heard the silence and came peeking through the kitchen doorway where Chick was standing, staring at Charlie. The scene made Margie think of a diorama in a wax museum. Chick said, "Charlie, what the hell are you doing?"

Charlie said, "Stirring the sauce. You want a taste?"

No one said a word. Then Charlie made his announcement. "Margie thinks it's rude behavior for all the men to sit while all the women cook." He tried to explain further. "Since cooking is hard work." He gave up on explaining and shrugged. "So I offered to help. If I didn't Margie would have stayed home."

Chick looked at his sister. "Is that all right with you?"

Palma said, "All I want is for Charlie and Margie to be happy." One broken engagement for Charlie was plenty for her.

Chick said, "Okay then."

The tension settled, and the kids dispersed, gazing over their shoulders at Margie, awed.

A little while later when Margie was in the dining room trying to set up a high chair, Denny O'Neill came in carrying two beers—one in each hand. Both beers were his. Margie smiled at him. She figured he was going to offer to help her with the high chair. She had no idea how to open it. He brushed by her and said into her ear, "I wonder what it'll be like—married to a faggot."

His face was an inch from hers. She didn't look away. She said, "Lush."

He left the dining room.

The next Sunday, Denny wasn't in his chair. He was upstairs, supposedly sleeping off a good one. Charlie called out from the kitchen into the living room, "Conversation's a lot raunchier in here." Palma rolled her eyes and then said to Charlie, sternly, something that sounded like "a spat."

Margie asked Mike's wife, "What's that mean?"

She said, "It means 'knock it off' in her dialect."

"What dialect?"

"*Bruzzese.*"

"*Broots-Aze?*"

"It's a place in Italy."

"Oh."

When dinner was ready, Charlie's oldest brother, Frank, came into the kitchen and took an enormous platter of chicken out of Palma's hands. There were twelve cut-up chickens on it. He said, "I got that, Ma." He headed for the dining room and dropped the platter. It didn't break because it was aluminum. It made quite a noise, though, and the children all crammed into the kitchen to gape. Margie leaped up to do something. Frank said, "Well, I guess you kids better help *Margie* pick up the chicken."

Margie said, "Can we rinse it all off?"

It turned out to be Palma who laughed first. Now the kids gaped at the adults, who were all laughing instead of being angry. Then the thrilled children got to put the chicken pieces into the sink and run water over them. Palma dipped the pieces into the tomato sauce and put them back on the platter. She waved the back of her hand at her guests and said, "I'll carry this." That got another big laugh, and Margie said, "I'm really sorry, Mrs. O'Neill."

Then Chick said, "That's what happens, kid, when you get yourself engaged to a faggot."

Palma said, "*Aspat!*"

Then they all tried not to laugh, but couldn't. Now Margie was in awe. They all *knew* what Denny O'Neill had said to her. She didn't know how they could have, but they did. Margie didn't understand the psychodynamics of a big extended family. At the table, sitting next to Chick, she said to him, "*Faggot* is not a very nice word. There are children here." She said it with a smirk.

Chick said, "Jesus H. Christ, kiddo, one cause at a time."

Then he gave her a mighty bear hug. Over his shoulder, at the corner of the table next to the high chair, Margie watched Palma spooning a bowl of pastina into a baby's mouth. But Palma's eyes kept wandering to the ceiling. Denny O'Neill did not abide crashing aluminum platters.

Besides reading, Margie spent her marriage acting as Charlie's secretary, keeping all the records that represented his obsessed journey toward finding the person who torched the Barnum & Bailey big top in Hartford, Connecticut, on July 6, 1944, killing 169 people, injuring 2,000 more, and leaving an angel-child unclaimed. Margie's short-lived job at the Travelers had proven expedient. With Margie by his side, Charlie's search became such a thorough one that eventually they would find Clayton T. Bart, whose thumbprint was in Margie's back. For Charlie to have come up with Clayton T. Bart left no doubt in anyone's mind that Charlie was scouring the ends of the earth for his arsonist.

Before Margie had come on the scene, he had already interviewed hundreds of witnesses to the fire—survivors, circus people, the Barbour Street neighborhood folks, firemen, psychiatrists, prisoners. Once married to Margie, he was able to hunt more efficiently, not only because of the secretarial skills she'd picked up at the Travelers, but also because of the Cadillacs. Every other year, she'd sell a Cadillac and they'd have the money to pay for the hundreds of telephone calls and the payments to various private detectives all over the country tracking down witnesses.

When they bought a house, one of the upstairs bedrooms became the war room. At least, Margie called it the war room. Charlie called it the den. In his "den," Charlie had an entire wall of loose-leaf binders labeled by date, starting with the first one, July 7, 1944, which represented the day after the fire. There were over a dozen books for July 6 itself. Charlie knew what was in each book by looking up the date in a little black guide he'd created. If computers had been available back then, Charlie would still have had to have all the space in his den. That's because the longest wall with no windows was papered with a blown-up, bird's-eye photo of the circus tent without the top that was referred to as "the Map." The view was accurately scaled. It was the view the Flying Wallendas had had from their little perch high above the center ring at the top of the tent, where they were standing when they first caught sight of the spot of flame.

After he had papered the photo onto the wall, Charlie surveyed it while he and Margie shared a bottle of wine. As he gazed upon his handiwork, he told her a story. "Margie, honey, in that moment, the first moment of the fire, Karl Wallenda thought of trying to save their bike. He'd designed it himself. He was the first tightrope walker to ride a bike across the tightrope. The bike cost a lot of money to have built. But then his next thought was that he wouldn't be able to save himself if he tried to hold the bike while he slid down the ladder. It weighed over a hundred pounds. He'd already ordered his family down the ladder even before the band broke into the 'Stars and Stripes.' He left the bike."

Margie asked, "Why didn't they just jump into the net?"

"No net."

"God. They didn't have a net?"

"Not the Wallendas." He settled Margie into the crook of his arm. "It's their theory that relying on a net makes the act foolhardy. The balancing poles weigh forty pounds. With this seven-man pyramid they're trying, they figure the poles and chairs will kill them in a fall. And they're so high up they'd bounce off the net anyway."

"Still, it seems like they'd have a better chance if they fell."

"But they don't fall. They practice on a rope ten feet off the ground and they don't try a stunt in a performance till they know they won't fall. If they can go a thousand times without falling, they know they're okay. Without that crutch—a net—they can't take anything for granted. Without a net, they won't fall. That's what they say, anyway."

He poured more wine. He explained to Margie that John Philip Sousa's "Stars and Stripes Forever" was a circus signal that meant clear the tent. He said, "The only time the 'Stars and Stripes' is ever played at the circus is when the audience is in danger. If a tiger escapes from a performance cage, the trainer pretends it's part of the act. Capturing the tiger becomes part of the act. When an animal gets out, circus people don't consider the audience to be in danger—only themselves, as always, so the march doesn't sound. But when there's a fire . . . "

Charlie and Margie sipped the wine, and they cuddled each other, and then they went to bed. The next day, the Wallendas fell. And no troupe of tightrope walkers would ever try the seven-man again.

★   ★   ★

Every year, on the anniversary of the fire, Charlie would put an ad in the Hartford *Courant* asking people who'd been to the circus to call him. He saw to it that the ad was placed next to the picture of Little Miss 1565 and the photo of Chick and his partner putting their latest bunch of flowers on her grave. AP would pick up the story, and often, in newspapers all over the country, little articles would appear about her, as well as mention of Charlie's search and the O'Neills's phone number. And every year more people would call, particularly the children who had been at the circus. As they grew up and came to see the ad, they wanted to talk. Margie became convinced that a repressed memory—a memory repressed for twenty or thirty years—could be recalled even more vividly than the memory of what you had for breakfast an hour ago. These people revealed their day at the circus when they were children in a way that made her think of floodwater gushing up out of a drain.

At first, Charlie paid his witnesses fifty dollars plus expenses, an amount that increased over the years, but did not mention the payment in the ad. He didn't want any more fakers than could be avoided.

The 1944 Hartford firemen figured that of all the people who tried to climb over the animal chute in order to get out of the main entrance, only a dozen or so made it, Margie included. Mostly children who were passed up by their mothers—mothers whom they would never see again. Also, an elderly couple dragged over by Hermes as he scaled the chute himself. But none of that dozen answered Charlie's ad. He said that was okay, since they wouldn't remember much of anything as they'd been the worst injured. That was not what he meant, though. Charlie had feelings of great compassion. He knew how impossibly painful it would be for that group of people to act as witnesses.

But many others came, and Charlie would introduce himself and Margie, and in the years to come, their girl, Martha, if she was underfoot. Then he'd ask them to describe the day as it began. The day as it began was no good to Charlie, but it warmed them up. They seemed to love talking about how excited they'd been, and how much they had anticipated going to the circus. Then they'd stop, look at Charlie, and wait. Not wait to be cued, Margie didn't think, but rather they'd wait as if in hope that something would now come along to interrupt them; they wanted the Archangel Gabriel to appear and say, "The rest is all a dream—it didn't really happen." But, alas, no Gabriel. Instead, they got Charlie, who said, "And when you got to the circus, what happened?"

So then they would tell about their amazement at the size of the tent; their trepidation as they passed the cage of the giant gorilla; their unease at the sideshow with the bearded lady, the mermaid, and the Elephant Boy; then about standing impatiently in line and getting inside and looking for their seats. Now Charlie would ask them to show him on the Map exactly where those seats were. They'd get up, walk across the room, and touch their seats on the Map with a very tentative index finger. Margie always felt relieved when they'd point to a place far away from Grandstand A. Then Charlie wrote their names on the Map, and the date of the interview, directly on squares representing the seats.

After all that, they'd give their versions of the wild animal act, the chill they felt as the big spot flashed on, capturing the Wallendas towering high above them about to walk out onto the tightrope, and then, the little spot of fire, a circle— as if someone had flipped a cigarette into the side of the tent. Charlie would slow them down at this point, asking them the route they had taken to get out of the burning tent because if he didn't, their next sentence would be, "We ran." So the route they described was always combined with descriptions of terrible panic: massive hysteria; wooden chairs crashing down the grandstands; pieces of burning canvas falling everywhere, falling on them; their clothes catching on fire; their hair sizzling; their skin burning; the unspeakable smell. And through it all, the resounding "Stars and Stripes."

When his witnesses finished speaking (they usually finished with the line, "I made it out"), Charlie would have them show on the Map their route and where they were positioned once outside the tent. They'd stand at the Map trying to explain to Charlie that there was a lot of chaos and that it was a long time ago, but this was the route, " . . . and this looks about where I ended up. Yes. Right here."

Then Charlie would ask, "Did you see anything you thought was peculiar? Once you were safely outside?"

That question usually got a variation on the answer "Yeah, man, I saw something peculiar. I saw a circus tent the size of the state capitol all on fire—going up like a pile of dry straw. Real peculiar."

Then Charlie would ask them to think past the horrible thing they'd witnessed, in hopes of hearing something that was Charlie's brand of peculiar. But there was never anything more to hear. Yet. That's what Charlie would say to Margie when she'd bring up that hurdle. "Yet."

He plodded on, year after year, while Margie sequestered herself, read books, and while their daughter Martha came into herself. Charlie and Margie named their baby after her dead grandmother. Charlie insisted, just as Jack Potter had insisted to his young wife in a letter. *Give the baby your own name. I'll have two Marthas. I'll be doubly happy.*

It wasn't until Margie came to have a baby that she understood as her father did why her mother took her to that sprawling tent jammed with people on such a hot day. It was because babies are boring. They do nothing. Good mothers take their babies to sit in the park or to be pushed in baby swings or out for strolls. Those things were incredibly tedious to Margie, and she imagined they had been tedious to her mother. She felt a real connection to her own mother for the first time when she had a baby of her own. Margie held her daughter and dreamed of the original Martha holding her— loving her—but not willing to give up what was fun for her, all alone, without her husband. As if my mother, thought Margie, could stand to push a baby around in a stroller, day in and day out, or talk to a baby who couldn't understand what she was saying and wouldn't be able to hold up her end of the conversation even if she could understand it.

In the sixties, when people had pet rocks, Margie didn't think that was so wild and crazy. "Pet rock" pretty much described a baby, except a rock lets you sleep at night. Because of that attitude, and because Charlie wanted only two things in life—finding out who set the fire and pleasing Margie—they took their baby everywhere they wanted to go, just the way Margie's mother had done. To a baby, Fenway Park is no less boring than any other park. Sitting in the stands, Margie and Charlie would take turns holding Martha and giving her a bottle. At one game, there was a ceremony retiring number 9. They joined in the standing ovation, jug- gling the baby, and Charlie lifted his child up over the crowd and told her that she was seeing the greatest hitter in baseball. The baby didn't hold up her end of that conversation, either, but so what? Margie and Charlie were having a grand time, and subsequently, so was she. Margie wondered if babies real- ly had any fun when their activities put their parents in a pall.

They took her to play golf, too. Charlie pulled the cart with the clubs and Margie pulled the cart with the baby. Of course, Margie was only nineteen years old, and energetic and fun-loving, perhaps not an age to expect a girl to have the frame of mind to be a responsible mother, but she made the baby fun. And Charlie was not a teenager, and recognized that raising a baby took at least two people, so he made the job as easy as he could for Margie, in addition to the fun.

Margie would have taken her daughter to the circus, too, if there had been one. But the circus didn't come back to

Hartford for a long time, and when it did it was the Shrine Circus, not Barnum & Bailey, and the show was held in the state armory, not in a tent. There's nothing more fireproof than a building made of blocks of New Hampshire granite with nothing in it—no need to store arms once the war had ended. But whoever made that decision to hold the first returning circus at the state armory didn't know that the building had been the site of a temporary morgue for the Barnum & Bailey Circus fire victims. When Charlie's family learned there'd be a circus at the armory, Chick said, "Whenever I go by that place, I see bodies." The best books Margie read, she felt, were the ones that had the greatest amount of irony. She couldn't think of a match for the irony in holding the first circus to come to Hartford in twenty years at the armory.

Charlie didn't want any more babies after Martha. That was okay with Margie. Martha interfered with her reading quite a bit. Her plan, to have babies so she could just sit around and read, had been unrealistic. With the baby, she found, all her activities, and her train of thought, too, were continually interrupted. But she was an only child and she figured she'd been very happy, so why shouldn't Martha be a happy only child, too? Margie's cousin, Little Pete, was an only child, and he was very happy. Although when he grew up and got married, he had a great slew of babies one after the other. He shared them with Margie because they continued to do a lot of things together, Little Pete and her and all those kids. Charlie's hours were often very long. Martha was three years older than Little Pete's first, and Martha would later say, "The reason I'm so successful is because I'm the eldest of seven children." Margie would think that she and all these pop psychologists around were probably right. But she would also think that maybe watching Ted Williams at Fenway Park instead of ducks ratting around a pond may have helped, too.

Chapter Five

Most of the people who came to the war room had scars—a seared arm or a streak across a cheek—left by the burning pieces of canvas, which not only rained down upon them, but had also stuck to them as they fled the tent. When the weapon napalm gained a reputation, Charlie said, "That's what we had at the circus." These people with the scars seldom took the money. They were grateful finally to be able to talk, and they wanted to help Charlie find the person who did this to them. Sometimes they said that: I want to know who did this to me! The ones with the burns believed, without reservation, that the fire was the work of an arsonist. Margie said, "They know so many little details." Charlie answered, "Yeah." And then she said to him, "You know, they really seem to need to blame someone." He gave her a look, as if she were speaking a foreign language.

"Margie, of course they want to blame someone. Some bastard ruined their lives. Someone is at fault. They blame him. Why wouldn't they?"

Margie tried to point out that these people's lives weren't actually ruined, but he didn't seem to want to hear that. The thought of ruined lives served as more impetus to him. So she didn't press it though she felt uneasy.

Margie tape-recorded Charlie's witnesses, but sometimes she had to leave the room when the scarred people talked. They talked of the feelings of getting torn from their mothers, getting crushed, getting smothered, getting burned. They described the smell of the noxious burning canvas and their charred skin. It made Margie queasy to have to think that this was what her mother experienced before she suffocated.

One of Charlie's questions was, "What did you hear?"

"Screaming and the band playing," they'd say. It was the circus music that prodded their struggle to get out of the tent, and what calmed them as well, once they'd made it out. But beyond the screams they described, and the racket of folding chairs clattering down the bandstand, they never went on to describe the sounds a fire makes, the ones Charlie and his firemen friends talked about all the time: the cracking and popping, crunching and sizzling; the whoosh of sucked-up oxygen; the wheeze of the trailing wind left behind. Just like the survivors of the *Titanic*, they heard music. At the circus, the Merle Evans Circus Band, the best there ever was, didn't go down with the ship, but they waited until the last possible moment before they got the hell out— when the center pole began to fall. The musicians held their instruments under their arms, ran as hard and as fast as they could, and set up again just past the line of killing heat, and kept on playing. A new song now. Some people would actually hum "The Pennsylvania Polka" for Charlie because they didn't know the title. "The Pennsylvania Polka" held no special circus meaning; Merle Evans chose it because he always felt it was the most cheerful tune ever written.

A few of the circus fire survivors were especially memorable, their visits cause for excitement. And so, the excitement Charlie felt after getting a call from Alfred Court's assistant so saturated the air of their house that little Martha, who was five at the time, acted the way she would if a big snowstorm had been predicted. On the day the famous animal trainer's underling was to arrive, Margie couldn't drag Martha away from the window where she waited and watched. And Margie herself felt the same way she did when she was getting near the end of *The Spy Who Came in from the Cold.* She'd actually missed the plane to a firefighters' convention when she had been on her way to meet Charlie in Los Angeles. She had been sitting right by the gate at La Guardia and she missed every call, including the last one. She had finished the book, closed it with a great sigh, looked at her watch and rushed over to the little podium where an American Airlines clerk was putting together papers, and asked, "Did the plane leave?"

He said, "You've got an hour, ma'am."

She was so relieved. She said, "The flight's really late then."

He said, "Nope. On time." Then he flashed her an airline-personnel smile. Margie looked behind his head at the departures board. He had been talking about a flight to Chicago. Her flight to California was long gone.

Alfred Court's assistant wore a red cape. She sashayed in the door, threw off the cape, and Charlie rushed to catch it. The woman was a knockout until she was up close; Margie could see the face-lift places and the wrinkles that weren't lifted under her tan-colored makeup. Her platinum hair was a mountainous wig, and the smile—the same bright red as the cape—was dazzling. She was a voluptuous showgirl, past middle age, whose complexion was stiff with makeup and rosy rouge, her curled eyelashes heavy with thick layers of black mascara. She was one of those nameless assistants whose job might be to parade across a stage with a headdress of feathers, or to let her body be sawed in half, or, in the case of the Barnum & Bailey Circus, to strike a pose while Alfred Court put his head in a lion's mouth. She had the look that Dolly Parton later said she aspired to as a child. The woman's name was Dixie. That's how she introduced herself. She stuck out her hand and said, "The name's Dixie. That's all there is. Like Cher."

Margie was afraid Martha might end up aspiring to the same ideal, she was so mesmerized. Before Martha had to go off to her afternoon kindergarten, she got to shake Dixie's hand. She said, "Pleased to meet you." And Dixie said, "Likewise." Then Martha said, wearing her longest face, "I have to go to school now." And so Dixie whipped out from her big bag an eight-by-ten glossy of herself wearing sequins and spangles, entwined in the trunk of an elephant rearing back on his hind legs. She signed it for Martha, and said to her, "You can show this to your little pals."

The preliminary excitement of having a person come to the O'Neills' who was not only a celebrity—well, kind of a celebrity—but who also had been in and out of the burning tent while remaining in complete control was nothing compared to the tension that grew and grew as Dixie spoke. Dixie turned out to be Charlie's first concrete evidence that there might have been a firebug. Concrete, yet flimsy, Margie thought. Though Margie was always willing to suspend her disbelief for Charlie just the way she did for John Le Carré, she was pretty cynical.

Besides her success at posing in such a way as to dramatize Alfred Court's feats, Dixie also proved to be equally competent in an emergency. In the first moments of the fire she was the one who got the last of the big cats through the chute and into their string of wagons lined up outside the tent before they could panic and run back to where they came from, as frightened animals are apt to do—as frightened humans are apt to do, too. Margie, married to a fireman, had learned that dead people in burning houses were always found in their closets or under their beds. Charlie came home on those nights and would head straight to the war room, where his circus arsonist represented all arsonists, represented negligent landlords, kids playing with matches, old people with twelve electric cords plugged into one outlet. Margie couldn't console him on those nights, only his search could. If she tried, she would only end up feeling frustrated. And annoyed.

Dixie said, "I had half the animals out when I looked up and saw it starting. Up above me. Up the side of the tent. I sped 'em along. I said, 'Hurry, hurry, hurry you pretty boys and girls.' I called 'em that." She sighed and smiled. "My cats." The smile dissolved. "So Vickie and her two babies were the last ones out. Found I had to hose the three of 'em down. Singed."

Charlie said, "And they were?"

"Leopards. Took a month before their spots looked normal again. Wish I could have done more, mister. More than just that."

"You prevented a bigger catastrophe, ma'am."

"Dixie."

"Dixie."

She sighed again. "Don't know about that. People get off thinking about what it'd been like if the animals were loose. Just would've been sadder is all. Cats would've slunk together in a huddle and burned. But what I do know is I was hosing down Vickie and her babies while the people up against the chute were dying. 'Course I know I shouldn't feel as bad as I do—my little bitty hose couldn't have done a thing for that tent. See, it was attached to the animals' drinking tank. Couple of gallons is all." She looked to Charlie.

"I understand."

"But I still feel bad. Keep on thinking that if the act ended just a minute sooner, I'd have spotted that fire right when it started—maybe could've gotten it out."

"You couldn't have," Charlie said. "The canvas was coated with gasoline."

"I know." She pushed up the sleeve of her dress and there was a skin graft peeking out. "Anywho, I didn't even think to hose myself down. Piece of canvas blew into me. Stuck right on to my shoulder." She dropped the sleeve and patted the spot. She looked up, "The paraffin."

Charlie asked, "What did you do after you hosed down the leopards, Miss . . . ?"

"I told ya, honey. Just Dixie."

"Sorry."

"S'okay. I went and stood by Gargantua. Knew he'd be upset. We had him over in his sideshow cage not too far from the main entrance so's everyone could get a gander at him on the way into the big top. I just kept talking and talking to him while everyone was running from the tent. The heat of it was fierce. I never stopped talking till the tent finished burning. Took about five minutes, no more. That tent was a big sucker. Twice the size of our tent today. Five minutes and it was gone." She snapped her fingers. Her fingernails were long and painted. Margie hadn't ever seen a red as red as that.

Something began to form in Charlie's eyes. Up till now he hadn't spoken to anyone who'd actually stood watching the whole thing. Up till now everyone had been running away or they were being burned or crushed, or they were busy helping the hysterical children separated from their mothers, and the just-as-hysterical mothers who were searching for their children.

Charlie asked, "Did you see anything unusual?"

Now Dixie squinted at Charlie. "Well . . . 'course I was

concentrating on Gargantua . . . but everyone was doing the same thing which I guess you'd call unusual. They were all running away from the burning tent, afraid to so much as take a quick glance back. Even when they stopped running, they didn't look back. Lot of 'em just put their faces in their hands.

"The screaming was what made Gargantua crazy. He stood there gripping the bars of the cage like there was no tomorrow—shaking them till I thought he'd rip 'em out. In the papers, reporters said he was trying to escape from the fire. Horsetrash! He knew he was safe. He'd always trusted me. Some jackass even said the gorilla was laughing, getting his revenge. But no sir, not Gargantua. What he was doing was begging me to let him out so he could save those screamin' kids. He loved children."

Dixie stopped talking and Charlie remained silent. Margie closed her eyes. For a moment, their minds were off dead children while they felt sorry for a gorilla. Then Charlie asked, "And what did you do next . . . Dixie?"

"Next, I went to my wagon, melted down a pot of Vaseline, and saturated the piece of canvas with it." She stopped and took in their confusion. "See, I didn't notice the canvas stuck to me till I was walking back to my wagon wondering why the hell my shoulder felt so stiff. Skin came off with it, though. 'Fraid of that." She lifted up her sleeve again. "Got this graft in Chicago. Not bad, huh?"

"It looks good," Margie said.

"You were burnt too, right?" She gazed at Margie. People had come to think that Charlie's obsession had to do with his falling in love with the girl whose whole back was burned in the fire. Margie just kind of went along with that assumption. She said, "Yes, I was."

"Sorry."

"Thank you."

Dixie said, "You get grafts?"

Margie cleared her throat. "No, I didn't."

"How come?"

Charlie was staring at her. Margie said, "I never saw the need."

There was a silence. Then Dixie said, "They come a long way, honey. Give me a call if you want the name of my man. His family's circus. His specialty is circus. Fixes broke bones, clawed skin, rope burns. Told him a rope burn wasn't as bad as what I had, but he said not to worry. So I didn't. He was damn good. I was able to rip all those little puffy sleeves off of my costumes soon's he took off the bandages. Amazin'."

Margie thanked her again.

Dixie said to Charlie, "Really think someone started that fire, don't ya?"

"Yes, I do."

"Hate to think you're right, mister. At the same time, I never heard of a circus tent catchin' fire all by itself. But I can't help you there. When you're keepin' a gorilla calm, you don't concentrate on much else."

Charlie leaned forward in his chair. Dixie did, too, though she didn't know it. Charlie's eyes could draw a person to him like he had the person on a leash. Those eyelashes. He said, "Dixie, you were just outside the tent. Fifty feet from where the fire started. Who else was there?"

"Nobody."

"Are you sure?"

"'Course not. Who could be sure?"

"I guess it isn't necessary for me to ask you to think about it."

She pressed her lips together. "No, sir, it ain't. Many a night I lay in my bed thinkin' about not much of anything else. But I'm ready, now, to do some extra thinkin'. Haven't been ready to do that till now; that's why I come. Waited till I could take the sleeves off my costumes. See, I believe I know someone who could help both of us. Help me with my thinking and help you too, mister."

"Not mister. Charlie."

Her face had been so pained. Now she smiled. She said, "Charlie."

"And who would that person be?"

"That would be the Master of Illusion."

She paused, still smiling, grinning actually. She was a flirt and she was also a performer. She knew all about dramatic timing.

Charlie said, calm as could be, "The Master of Illusion?" as if someone had suggested him before.

"That's right. He's a clown, a magician, too. He comes out into the ring, snaps his fingers, and puffs of pink smoke come out of the snap. And he's a contortionist. Fits in a car that's no more than two foot square."

"How could he help us?"

"He's a hypnotist, too. The best. Off season, he does night-clubs and things like bowling banquets and bar mitzvahs. Gets people to act like they're chickens. 'Course, then he's known as the Master of Hypnosis. He's a real psychologist, honest to Pete. Went to school. He can get people to stop smoking, things like that. But he's circus. He gets real bored out there. Can't wait to come back."

"He could get me to remember whatever it was I forgot after all these years. He'll do it for me because I stand in as his assistant once in a while—when his wife is having babies. They got about eight or nine kids, that's why he has to work outside."

"How do you assist him?"

"I get to open the car door."

"And what's this hypnotist's name?"

"Told ya. The Master of Illusion."

"I mean his real name."

"Real name's Bud. He kind of likes Master, though."

The tape broke. It didn't matter. With a nod from Charlie

toward the phone, Alfred Court's assistant was hooked up with the Master of Illusion in just a few minutes. He was working at a club in Boston. She exchanged some polite talk, asked for his family, and then told him what she was about. Then she put her hand over the phone and said, " 'Course he wants a thousand big ones. Me and him will split."

Charlie looked over at Margie. Margie said, "Why not?" The thought of watching this woman get hypnotized thrilled her. She listened as Dixie and her friend spent half an hour shooting the breeze about their last performance together, laughing, and later, when she'd left, Charlie and Margie kidded around themselves—talked about subtracting the phone bill from the thousand.

Margie said to Charlie, "It could be a scam."

"It is a lot of money, Margie."

"Who cares about money? But these people aren't known for honesty, right?"

"You're thinking of carnies, honey. Not circus people."

"Well . . . let's do it. Time to sell the old Caddie anyway. It must have at least seven hundred miles on it."

Charlie kissed her. She kissed him back. He said, "We've only got twenty minutes till Martha gets back."

"Then you'd better make it good."

Margie wanted to invite everyone they knew to the hypnosis session, but Charlie reminded her that it wasn't exactly a party. When Charlie would remind her of what he was actually up to, it would dawn on her that though his firebug hunt might be a game for her, it was no game for him. Margie had a living thriller going on in a private corner of her house— she was in the middle of a best-seller, married to Nero Wolfe, or Hercule Poirot, or even Sherlock Holmes, all those detectives who never wanted wives. Margie's detective wanted one—wanted Margie. She asked Charlie if Martha could sit in.

At this stage, Martha had gotten to be a real friend to her parents, holding up her end of the conversation. She loved being read to, and she was just learning to read herself. Now, Margie was reading the *Odyssey* to Martha, a chapter a night. She loved gore, as did her mother. Reading the poetry that they couldn't understand geared them up for all Homer's gore, which they could.

Charlie agreed to let Martha sit off in a corner while the Master hypnotized Dixie. So Margie explained what hypnosis was to her daughter beforehand. Margie told her it was *real* magic as opposed to make-believe magic like in the *Odyssey*. Martha said, "Make-believe?" And Margie had to backtrack and explain that there wasn't any such thing as a giant with a big eye in the middle of his forehead.

Martha said, "But I bet there are Sirens."

Margie said, "Well, there are whirlpools, that's for sure."

Martha shivered. "I know. Right down the drain." Then she did an imitation of a drain, though she looked more like a person sucking up spaghetti.

Charlie warned Martha that the lady might say some really sad things about what she saw when the circus burned down.

Martha said, "About Mommy's back getting burned?"

"Well, yes, she'll talk about all kinds of people getting burned."

"About the little girl that got burned that no one knows who she is?"

"That's right."

Martha's eyes sparkled. She couldn't wait. Neither could Margie. And neither could Charlie.

Chapter Six

They both wore capes except that the Master's was black. After Dixie had made the introductions, and they'd shaken hands, the Master of Illusion stooped down by Martha, reached out to her, and said, "Now what's this in your hair?" And he pulled a tiny paper butterfly out of one of her curls. Martha was agog and immediately felt in her hair for more. He said, "Just this one," and he put it into her hands. Margie said to him, "You really are a master of illusion." He said, "Well, we all are, aren't we? It's just that circus people can't let themselves get carried away."

The Master didn't swing a watch on a chain. He hypno-tized people with his voice. Martha was sitting next to Margie by the tape recorder. Thirty seconds after he started hypnotizing Dixie, Margie noticed Martha swaying. She caught her and put her to bed. Margie whispered to Charlie,

"I hope I won't have to spend another thousand in the morning getting the Master of Illusion to wake this kid up."

When she got back into the room Dixie was chatting away and Margie thought that they were waiting for her. Then she realized that Dixie was talking to an invisible point in the air about a foot above the Master's head. She was back in time, back at the circus describing what she saw of the catastrophe as it was happening: " . . . and then the Wallendas went right to their wagons except for Hermes; he's the youngest. He stayed for a minute or two to pull a few kids over the chute. I'll tell ya, the Wallendas were strange birds. Kept to themselves. Couldn't speak any English whatsoever. Don't know what they spoke. Someone asked them once if they were Hungarian and that bent them all out of shape. They're Gypsies. 'Course I wasn't born circus, so I never could understand why Gypsies aren't something besides Gypsies. I mean, it's not like there's a Gypsyland somewhere."

The Master interrupted her with his serene voice. "And tell me what happened, Dixie, after the Wallendas had gone back to their wagon."

Dixie's brow wrinkled. She said, "Well, the clowns' faces were melting. Emmett was late for his act because he'd been trying to keep his nose on. I'm not talking about the fire, now. This was before the fire. Y'see, once the temperature goes over ninety degrees, makeup melts. Right from the start it was a damn, hot, sorry day. But anyway, Emmett is supposed to do his all-alone act to divert the crowd while the cage comes down and while the Wallendas climb their ladder. First, the cats rouse them, then Emmett mopes around making them feel real sorry for him, and then—boom— goosebumps; there's the Wallendas in the big spot at the tippity-top of the tent. Magic. And ya know what? When thousands of people say 'oooooh' all at the same time, I get a shiver.

"But that day, Emmett was late because he couldn't keep

his nose on, so the crowd was watching the roustabouts dismantle the cage. 'Course the audience is just supposed to see the magic. A lion is there in front of you, and then before you know it, he's gone, and there go five people, high in the sky, all piled up on top of one another riding a single bike on a steel cable that the crowd thinks is a rope. Magic. That's what the circus is."

The Master said, "When did you finally spot Emmett?"

"I saw him outside running to the tent while I was just getting ready for the last of 'em, Vickie and her babies. I saw Emmett, and right then, I saw a little bit of fire on the side of the tent. Then the little fire ripped up the tent, and then I heard Merle switch to the 'Stars and Stripes.' So then I had to concern myself getting Vickie out—she'd stopped at the 'Stars and Stripes.' I said, 'Vickie, you come on, honey.' When she came through she was frantic, but the babies were right behind her. The canvas had started breaking up so they'd caught a few pieces. Had to cool them down." Dixie paused. Her eyes darted around. She pointed, "There he is now!" With that, Dixie leaped out of her chair and pointed at the window.

"Who?"

"Emmett! Praise Jesus. All the while I had this feeling that he'd run into the tent. That he'd never come out. And look at that! He's got a bucket! He's gonna try to put out the fire. Oh, Emmett! But I've got to get to that Gargantua. Vickie's okay, she's in her cage lickin' her babies. They're just fine. But Gargantua, what about him? He can't take any commotion. He's old now. Emmett's standing in the middle of the lot holding his bucket, but now he's turning away—looking toward me. His nose is gone. Everyone is turning away, same as Emmett. All of them, pouring out of the exits. But I got Gargantua now, and me and him are together watching it all.

"That's okay, big fella, that's okay. The children will be just fine—soon's those boys get them out. See, honey, they're getting all the children out right now."

Dixie had tears coursing down her cheeks through the tan makeup, leaving jagged white tracks. The Master asked her, "And what else is happening?"

"The whole tent is on fire. The whole tent. Those soldiers who passed the children are running. Hermes Wallenda is running to his trailer. His spangles are smoking. They're smoking! No, no, Gargantua, honey. See the children lying on the blankets? Look at Emmett making them laugh."

Then she stopped talking to the gorilla. She went back to the spot over the Master's head. "There are sirens all around us, but the fire trucks are here first and the ambulances can't get in. So people are taking the burned children down the street. Running with them. You can't leave burned people lying in the sun—not this hot sun we got here today."

The Master said, "Do you see a little baby girl that the soldiers got out of the fire?"

"Yes, sir! She's wearin' black shoes, and I'm wonderin'—now why the hell isn't she wearing those itty-bitty white baby shoes? 'Course, the shoes are covered with soot, stupid me. Gargantua sees her, too. He's makin' those little cheeping sounds he makes when he's feeling bad. His worry for the child is calming him, though. I think maybe he's singing to her. I'm telling him not to worry, the baby's going to be all right."

And Margie imagined not herself, but Martha, lying in the field, her back burned, her white baby shoes turned black. Charlie sensed what Margie must have been thinking, and he came over and took her out of her chair by her shoulders, sat down, and cuddled her into his lap. She was shaking like a leaf.

Now the Master asked what Charlie had prompted him to ask, and Margie felt Charlie grow tense. "What do you see that stands out most of all, Dixie?" And to Margie that question, for the first time, was so absurd. What that question really meant was: In all this horror and chaos, did anything look normal?

Dixie said, "I just see commotion now. And I hear the band. My God, they're still in the tent. *They're still in the tent!* Why don't they get out?" She started screaming, "Merle! Merle!" Then she shouted. "The pole! The pole is coming down."

Like almost every witness, she remembered the sound of her own voice shouting, "The pole, the pole!" and that was when everyone in the lot finally turned around to look for just a second, in time to see what was left of the tent collapse.

Dixie said, "Oh, mercy. Here they come! They're out! Merle and the musicians are settin' up over at the edge of the lot. They're all covered in soot. Their uniforms are supposed to be red, but they ain't red now. They're burned black. Their jackets have holes in them. Merle's jacket is smoking the way Hermes Wallenda's spangles were doing. They're playing 'The Pennsylvania Polka.' Lordy, that's always such a rouser."

Margie wondered if her mother died listening to Merle Evans's circus band playing their polka or maybe she was already dead before they'd finished the "Stars and Stripes."

"What do you see that is different from all the rest, Dixie?"

And calmly as could be, Dixie said, "Oh, just that kid who keeps watching the whole thing. Like me and the gorilla. He doesn't look the other way like everyone else. He just keeps watching. He steps back, but he doesn't run away. Then, when the sirens start, he's gone."

The Master said, "What else is different about him? There are lots of children running away."

"But they're all crying. Or screaming. For their mothers. They're looking for mama. Not him. The boy runs away down the street. None of the other children run away down the street. They're staying there calling for their mothers. And now there are lots and lots of children running *up* the street—children from the neighborhood, come to see the fire. The lot is filled with people—firemen and policemen and people. Some of the children run to the policemen."

Dixie had broken into a sweat. The same sweat she'd been in twenty years before. The Master looked to Charlie and Charlie nodded.

The Master took Dixie out of her trance by clapping his hands with a loud smack. Dixie looked away from her spot in the air and said to her friend, "This just ain't workin', is it sugar? But I tried."

The Master said, "It worked. You're all done."

Dixie looked over at Margie. "Hey, now, is that true?"

Margie said, "Yes. It's all right here on tape."

"Well, then, I'll be a red hen." Now she looked close at Charlie and Margie. "You two certainly got all cozy," and she saw that Margie was quivering a little. "Aw, honey. I upset you there, didn't I? I do apologize."

Margie said, "I'm okay."

"You sure?"

"Yes."

"I'm gonna want a copy of that tape. I hate the sound of my own voice—feel like I'm hearing my Ma—but the doc says I should hear it. I called him yesterday, I was so nervous. The doc who fixed my shoulder. Says I got to fix my brain, too. So I'll play that tape soon's I pick the right fella to cuddle me." And Charlie snuggled Margie even closer, which was an expression of sympathy for Dixie.

Later, that night, when Charlie and Margie were in bed, trying to fall asleep, they gave up and started talking and talking, hashing out all Dixie had said like two little kids in on a big secret. Margie said, "Charlie, would a child really set such a terrible fire?"

He said, "Happens every day. They don't know, though, what their fires are capable of." Charlie put out a lot of fires like that. Set by kids.

"So maybe it was a kid playing with matches after all."

"No. If a kid did it, he did it deliberately."

"You set store by what she said, right?"

"Right."

"But she didn't see him set it. The boy."

"No."

"So we don't know if a child set the fire."

"No, we don't."

"Charlie, we don't know anything, do we?"

Charlie said, "Lie down, Margie. We do know something. About bravery. It may not sound like much what Dixie did, hosing down the leopards. But she was standing in a furnace."

"I know that, sweetheart, but where does that get us?"

"The more we understand about what was going on, the more we'll see."

"But was that worth a thousand dollars?"

"It was, Margie. Because now I can ask everyone who's been here—send out postcards—ask if they saw a little boy standing and watching, not looking for his mother, and then running away. Maybe one of them will say, 'Yeah. I knew him.' Or, 'Yeah. I was that little boy.' And if that boy comes here to confess to us, I've done my job."

Charlie pulled Margie down to him and smiled at her in the dark. Charlie's smiles had never reflected happiness. He was a driven man, and Margie came to know that he wouldn't be happy until he got to where he was driving toward. So when he smiled a smile of affection for Margie, she decided it was more a smile of relief—remembering how he had her in his life. When Martha was being adorable, his smile was more like amazement—amazement that he also had someone as precious as his baby in his life, too.

Margie said, "Charlie, will you be happy once you find out who set the fire?"

He said, "I'm happy now, Margie." Then he said, "I want justice done. For your mother. For Dixie. And for these." He ran his hands over and across the ropes of scars covering Margie's back. She shuddered.

Chapter Seven

When Charlie was at work, and Martha at school, and Margie was home reading, or housecleaning, or chatting on the phone with the mothers of Martha's friends, sometimes she'd hear a siren. Once in a while that meant Charlie would come home from work with black fingernails, the only physical evidence that he'd fought a fire. Firemen work hard to wash themselves and their brains after a fire.

Charlie would walk in the door, sit at the kitchen table, and tell Margie there'd been a fatality, or that people had suffered terrible injuries. She'd bring him cough syrup. What helped him more than anything was sharing Martha, so Margie would tell him what she was up to and he'd eventually begin to relax. It was still the same as telling him "The Fox and the Grapes" on the raft at Chalker Beach. He loved to listen. Then he'd go unwind. He'd go to the war room, alone. That had always been okay with Margie. But she found she was glad and relieved that Martha did not inherit their need to be alone—Charlie when troubled, Margie because solitude just seemed nice. Margie found it so nice to squirrel away with a book. Viewing herself and her husband through Martha's eyes, Margie came to wonder at the amount of time Charlie continued to put into his search.

Even when Charlie went on field trips with Martha, always the only dad, he was still thinking about fires. Both Margie and Charlie went on the field trip to Farmington Avenue to visit Mark Twain's house. Martha was intrigued by the printing press Mark Twain had sunk his money into, money that was lost on the dinosaur of a machine that was not cost effective. Margie couldn't drag herself away from his desk where he'd written the books she so treasured. But Charlie the fireman was appalled at the writer's fireplace. Mark Twain, the dreamer, fantasized about a hearth blazing in the dead of winter with snow falling onto the flames. So he designed a fireplace with a soaring window over it, with two flues rising on either side of the glass. The children were all admiring, but Charlie told them about the dangers of a bent flue. "Creosote builds up in the elbow." He touched the angle in one of the flues. "Lucky he didn't kill himself and his whole family."

For a long time, between the ages of eight and twelve, Martha got all involved in his war-room work. The two would put their heads together once a week or so, and he'd go over everything with her; they'd peruse his reports and listen to the latest tapes. But when she got to be twelve, not only did she take on new adolescent interests, she also closed the door on her father's interests. His sole interest. At the dinner table one night, she said, "Well, Dad, I guess there's no conclusion to be drawn except that maybe there was an arsonist. But there's no way we're ever going to find out who he was, right?"

Martha smiled at her father. She was the captain of the junior high school debating team, the only seventh-grader, and the older kids had voted her captain. But whenever Charlie discussed the circus fire, there was no room for debate, so he said to her, "Oh there was one, Martha, and I'll find him."

She shrugged and dashed off. The mouths of babes, Margie thought. And, she thought, she and Charlie had a real smart babe who from then on began to see that what her dad was doing was weird. Martha started to break away, and it seemed that her goal was to take her mother with her. For her thirteenth birthday she asked for a trip to Boston, and it wasn't baseball season. She wanted to see the historical sights she was learning about in school and she wanted to do it with her mother. Martha enjoyed being needed. To her shock and disappointment, she'd found that her father didn't need her one bit. So she would work on Margie.

On the train to Boston, she told Margie how her class had learned about the Charter Oak, not only the spy-thriller aspect of the patriots hiding the charter from the British, but also about the tree itself and how environmentalists had tried to save it when it was dying. Margie remembered reading about that effort in the Hartford *Courant*; it was quite a few years back. "In those days," Margie explained to Martha, "everyone called environmentalists *bird-watchers*, so saving the tree didn't warrant much shrift."

Martha asked, "Mom, what's bird-watching got to do with saving the tree?"

Margie said, "The term *bird-watchers*, Martha, is derogatory. Kind of a degrading epithet for a conservationist. It means you're a sissy and maybe a little bit cuckoo."

Just from her expression, let alone the tirade to follow, Margie could see that progress in the face of destroying sacred trees would hold no charm for Martha's generation.

They had fun in Boston, though Martha kept bringing up the subject of her dad's stubbornness. Martha's worry over her father was deeper than Margie had suspected. Margie tried to soothe her and tell her that what her daddy did was sort of a hobby. Just like some dads who were always building shelves. In fact, Charlie built a few shelves himself. "Just for the war room, Mom." The tour guide at the Old North Church got a little annoyed with their whisperings.

Margie took Martha to Durgin Park for dinner, where the waitresses are famed for their rough manner and where diners eat at long, groaning boards hip-to-hip with strangers. Martha was shocked.

Margie said, "This is supposed to be a riot, Martha."

"Well it isn't. And we can't hear each other."

So they had their dessert in a nice quiet little tearoom, passing up the famous Durgin Park indian pudding; Margie would let Martha have her say. But it was more a lecture than a "say." Martha wanted to know why her mother wasn't worried about her father. Couldn't she see that he was spending more and more time in the war room? He didn't ever listen to ball games any more, let alone go to them. Margie had noticed. "It makes him happy, sweetheart."

Martha was appalled again. She said, "Happy? It's not a life, Mom. How could it be happy?"

When they got home, Charlie told Margie that her trip with Martha was actually good for him, as it allowed him to have a whole day alone—he'd gotten to review things he hadn't thought were important. Margie had no idea he'd had that day off. She assumed he'd have offered to come along to Boston if he wasn't working. Margie found crumbs in the war room. He'd had his meals there. That night, they lay in each other's arms and Margie told him stories about Boston. Palma had been far too busy keeping her husband appeased to go on jaunts with her children. But just when was it when Charlie stopped going on jaunts with his little girl?

Martha came to enjoy her mother's undemanding company more and more. The trip to Boston led to other trips over

Martha's high school years—they'd take the train to New York, to go to museums and art galleries and concerts. Martha also took Margie to quirky bookstores where she knew Margie would happily browse half the day. But the more Margie saw of the world that lay beyond the Hog River, the more she had to face up to the fact that she'd missed much bigger things than just the Mysterious Bookstore on Fifty-sixth Street where she'd gazed in awe at the author's autograph inside the cover of a first edition of *The Red-Headed League*. While everybody had been talking about civil rights and feminism and Vietnam for the last ten years, Margie had been watching the Master of Illusion hypnotize Dixie or sitting around reading *Jonathan Livingston Seagull*. The autograph brought tears to Margie's eyes, and she quickly wiped them away and carefully replaced the book in its special place. Martha watched, and her heart broke to think that her mother cried because she couldn't afford $250 for an autographed Sherlock Holmes since the Cadillacs were always spoken for. Martha asked the clerk if he'd hold the book for her. She figured it would take her six months to save up the money. The clerk assured her he would.

Margie was now referring to the war room as the Smithsonian. Not in a good-humored way. In a cynical way. There were now two walls of shelves rather than just one, and Charlie's energies received an added jolt because during this time, a new era in American justice emerged. The FBI made available a clearinghouse of fingerprints. Charlie kept talking about how terrific it was to be able to find a set of prints, put them into a computer, and determine immediately who they belonged to. Margie thought that was terrific, too, but not for a particularly concrete reason. Then she wondered at how she could be so dense, sometimes. Sometimes she thought she didn't have much imagination, which is why it was so exciting for her to read stories that people actually made up out of thin air. And why Charlie appealed to her so much. His imagination was so far-reaching that his ever-expanding quest would always be exciting. Despite Martha, Margie had kept telling herself that.

So after waiting for some time for Margie to take the initiative, Charlie finally gave up and asked her if she wouldn't mind having a photographer take a picture of the thumbprint at the bottom of her spine. Margie told him that yes, she would mind. He asked her why and she was honest with him, as she had always been. She told him that there was nothing personal about not wanting her scarred back photographed, it was just that she had no interest.

He said, "No interest?" Charlie could be dense, too, in his own way. She didn't answer him. Then he said, "Don't you want to know who saved your life?"

No, she didn't want to know that. She already knew. Lots of people saved her life, she felt, mostly her Aunt Jane. She had enough guilt not being able to repay her aunt for all she'd done. But at the same time, Margie couldn't hurt Charlie by saying such a thing because she loved him so much. So instead she said, "The scar is almost worn away. There are no ridges left."

And he said, so earnestly, so honestly, "But not after you're dusted with powder. Then they'll show up."

Charlie never said no to Margie. He gave her all she asked him for. He loved listening to her Martha tales, of their trips to Lincoln Center, and the free tour of Grand Central Station where you get the thrill of looking down from a hole in the ceiling to the floor 250 feet below. Charlie told Martha that the Wallendas knew that feeling when they stood, perched, high above the carpet of tanbark, high above the upturned faces of the audience. And he'd made a special glass case for *The Red-Headed League* for

Margie's birthday that year. Martha had been so touched when she'd shown her dad the book; he looked at the spidery crawl of the author's signature and said to his daughter, "There wasn't a *real* Sherlock Holmes?"

But Charlie no longer had an interest in actually doing the things Martha and Margie were doing because he was "too wrapped up," but he loved seeing it all through their eyes. Listening to their stories. So Margie couldn't betray him. She'd never led him to believe that she wouldn't take part in his search, so how could she pull the rug out from under him now? Okay, she decided, bring on the photographer. But even though she'd do this for Charlie, she still felt free to tell him what she was thinking. And so, Charlie and Margie had their first fight. While she explained her feelings, she referred to the witnesses as "specimens." She said, "Charlie, up until now, I never felt you thought of me as one of your specimens."

He said, "Specimens?"

"I don't want my name pinned on the wall."

He was confused. "You can't be on the wall. You were too young. No one knows exactly where your mother sat. But Margie, I haven't treated anyone who's come here like a specimen. I've treated them kindly."

She apologized. She dropped it. Afterward she knew she shouldn't have because she felt this little bit of resentment bubble up. Just because he didn't see her as one of his specimens didn't mean she wasn't one.

A police-photographer friend of Chick's came to photograph Margie's back. Chick had said, "Don't be embarrassed, Margie. This guy's seen it all."

She wasn't embarrassed. But she wouldn't let Charlie be in the room. Margie was having a tough enough time without risking letting loose any more bubbles. Martha had brought up several, and last summer, a whole bunch of them had escaped when Charlie and she and his brother,

Michael, and Michael's wife rented a cottage at Chalker Beach. The low sand dune bordering the marsh grass that had hidden Charlie and Margie when they lay by the creek the summer they'd met had grown. It was six feet higher. They all oohed and aahed, and Michael's wife said sand dunes were just like the kids—you can't see them grow, but they grew so fast you wondered how it could have possibly been so easily missed. The resentment rose up that vacation week because Charlie kept making notes on a little pad. Margie had said, "Charlie, can't you just let it alone for a week?" He said, "I can't risk losing anything."

The fourth night at the beach they had had to sleep in the gym at Old Saybrook High School because a hurricane had just skimmed Cape Hatteras instead of turning inland. It would hit the Connecticut shore around dawn. Though hurricanes can wreak havoc, they can come and go in just a few hours, and this one, as it turned out, lost most of its punch when it crossed Long Island. And since it hit Old Saybrook at low tide, flooding was minimal. The next morning, the two couples returned to the cottage. The sand dune was gone.

Margie and Mike's wife got some pails to collect whatever treasures the hurricane might have left on the beach. They walked along, and Margie looked over her shoulder to see Charlie sitting on a beach chair scribbling in his notebook.

Chapter Eight

The cop may have seen it all, but he stepped back just a tiny bit when he took the towel from Margie's back. Her eyes were closed, but she felt his flinch. It felt nice, though, having him dust the scars with his soft brush. He took several shots using just the light from the window, then a flash, then a big spotlight, then with a white umbrella next to her. With another brush, he dusted off the powder. He said, "The powder is just talc, Mrs. O'Neill. You don't have to worry about it." She still went and took a shower.

Margie didn't care to see all the pictures, just the close-up Charlie sent to the FBI. It looked like a thumbprint, all right. The ridges were as clear as the sandbar at the creek at low tide; the one that fed the dune. Charlie said, "The FBI will be able to find the man if he's still in the service. Or if he's a criminal."

Clayton T. Bart was still serving in the air force, though unfortunately, he was stationed in Japan. This, Charlie said, was going to be a job for Chick. Chick had traveled the country, across and back many times, looking for clues linked to the identity of Little Miss 1565. He knew how to look and where to look. Unlike the Little Miss, reaching Clayton T. Bart meant starting with a name rather than hoping to end up with one—a far sight simpler. Chick's wife, Aunt Annette, said, "Thank God that man's going to have something to do for a few days." He flew down to Washington and came back a few days later with all the info—Aunt Annette knew exactly how long it would take him.

After the war, Captain Bart had been a member of the occupying forces in Tokyo. At the end of a six-year stint, he came to think of Tokyo as home because he'd mastered Japanese easily—a natural skill he didn't know he had. Also, he loved the food, and, of course, he'd fallen in love with a Japanese girl. In the air force, he had reached the rank of captain and now served as military attaché to the U.S. ambassador.

When Chick arrived in Washington to start figuring out the best way to contact Captain Bart, the ambassador to Japan happened to be in Washington to launch an exhibition of Japanese-manufactured computer chips in the capital. That news was in the copy of the *Washington Post* that Chick had been reading on the shuttle. Chick called from his hotel. He went looking for the exhibition hall, figuring he could ask around to see if the ambassador's military attaché had accompanied him. The exhibit, it turned out, fit in a cardboard box. "I was expecting some kind of car show," Uncle Chick said. But the important thing was that the attaché was with the ambassador. This neat little coincidence saved Margie a wad of money. It would have cost two Cadillacs to send Chick to Japan.

So Chick found Captain Bart quite easily, and via his network of police buddies, got him on the phone, told him who he was, arranged a meeting, and at the meeting told him who Margie was. At lunch, Captain Bart then told Chick how he'd been at Brainard Field during the month of July, in 1944, learning to fly B-52s. Big B-52s, the ones with the huge bomb bays. He had had to report on the Fourth, the holiday, so was free the two days following. He had decided to go to the circus. He'd been just nineteen years old. Later, when she heard this, Margie thought: Same age as my mother. Then, Chick told Captain Bart about Charlie, and he agreed to be interviewed. Chick said into the phone, "Margie, you there?"

She was on the extension. "Yes."

He said, "Captain Bart can't wait to meet you."

"Yeah."

Margie thought: And wouldn't Miss Foss be disappointed to hear me still saying *yeah*, instead of *yes*. Miss Foss, there are times when all you can get out is a yeah, and the reason is that you can't bring yourself to agree. *Yeah* is not the same as *yes*.

Margie's Aunt Jane planned a big family gathering so everybody could meet Clayton T. Bart and thank him. Margie's family: Aunt Jane, Uncle Pete, Little Pete, and the kids; and Charlie's family, more than two dozen aunts, uncles, cousins, etc., filled the O'Neill house. They were all excited and thrilled that Margie was going to be meeting the man who saved her life, and they'd get to look on and share the thrill. Martha said to her mother, "You don't want to do this, right, Mom?"

Margie said, "I don't want to spoil everybody's fun."

Then Martha tried out some newly acquired advanced placement psychology. "Not even at the cost it will exact upon you?"

Since that was the kind of question a kid felt free to ask in those new times of expressing themselves, Margie wasn't taken aback. She'd been getting those kinds of questions from Martha quite a lot lately. She said, "I have a responsibility to be nice to people who love me, even if it's a sacrifice. Besides, the cost isn't so great. I'm just feeling a little uneasy, that's all."

The other thing that Margie was feeling—that she didn't really think of as a being a great cost—was worry. She was very worried about her father. But she was always worried about him, anyway, so what was the difference? Martha, who could hear her mother think, it seemed, said, "You don't need any more worry about Grandpa than you already have."

So Margie called her Aunt Jane to tell her she was worried about her father, and her aunt told her that her father was going along with the idea, and was in fact, planning to come to the party. Come to the party? He hadn't left his room in the veterans' home since 1963. Margie was good and uneasy now. And if she was uneasy, what was he? She decided to visit him.

Jack Potter was physically able to care for himself, but he chose not to. Once he no longer needed to care for Margie, he decided not to bother with himself, either. Once he saw his duty to his daughter as finished, he just sat back and began his wait to die. He would have died, too, if Margie and Charlie and Jane and Big Pete and Little Pete had left him alone. In fact, that was why they'd initially insisted he go to the home. Margie told him letting him die would be an awful thing for her to have on her shoulders. She didn't tell him about his granddaughter's thoughts. Once Martha had gotten out of the horseradish, she'd become bitter about her beloved grandfather. She told Margie he should have just committed suicide and been done with it. She said, "Mom, you have just as much of a burden with him being in the home." Martha, the haughty high schooler, accused her mother of taking a terrible punishment without questioning it, and she said, "What about me, Mom? He has a duty to me to be a regular Grandpa. Or do you think only women should have duties?" Margie told her just to drop it. Martha said, "You don't protect people by letting them be stubborn, Mom." Margie knew Martha was right, but told her that it was everybody's duty—men and women—to respect a father's wishes. Martha said, "Bullshit."

So Margie decided to fight back. "He did think of suicide once."

Martha said, "What?" and listened to Margie say those words again, then looked into Margie's wretched eyes. Martha started to cry. Margie was still the parent, and so she hugged Martha while she cried, even though she knew that she should be the one who was crying, who was getting hugged. Then Martha said, "You know, this is one fucked-up family."

Margie said, "I really can't handle that language coming from you."

"Sorry, Mom."

Margie was beginning to know what Martha pointed out was true even if she did choose to express it in such a vulgar way. Martha made sense to her, as did her father's psychiatrist, who attributed Jack Potter's behavior to the trauma of his war experience. Margie told the psychiatrist that her father had really loved her mother to the point of obsession. But the psychiatrist said, "We blame love for a lot of things. Actually, it's an easy way out. It protects us from having to deal with the real injuries."

Margie nodded at him, understanding. When she was in the sixth grade and her class was studying the three paragraphs in their social studies book devoted to World War II, she'd gone home and asked Jack Potter about his war experience. Her father's response was, "In June of 1944, New England lost fewer men on the beaches of France than Connecticut did at the circus a month later."

He had really said it to the wall across from his chair at the kitchen table. He'd heard Margie's question, but had forgotten where it was coming from. They were having dinner at the time. He'd cooked chicken wings. He and Margie didn't like vegetables. They were eating and reading. He was reading his papers and Margie was reading her comic books. She didn't read her library books at the kitchen table because she might drip chicken grease on them, and in those days the librarians would flip through the pages searching for damage before accepting returns.

When Margie got married and visited her father at his new residence, she'd sit across from him at the little table in his room where he was reading. She always brought a book so she could read while he went through his newspapers and magazines just the way they'd done every night at home until Margie left their apartment to marry. She'd sit for an hour or so and then when she'd get up to go, he'd say, "Thanks for visiting with me, Margie." On occasion, he'd speak to the wall while she was visiting, the way he had at home. Once he said, "I hope my eyes go last." He didn't say that because he cared so much about his reading, but because the hospital staff tended not to bother him while he read. If he wasn't reading they'd try to start a conversation.

Even though he was carrying on a wall monologue, Margie still said, "Now they have books on tape, Dad, in case your *ears* are the last to go."

He said, "You *listen* to stories that people tell—you *read* stories that people write. What is the sense in it?"

Yeah. What's the sense in anything, Dad? Margie wondered. He saw no sense in living the life he might have led. He just wanted to get life by him. Early on, Margie believed that without his wife, life was not life for her father, just like tapes were not books. Margie used to look at him and think: This man has a broken heart and there's no mending it. But as she came to know his new psychiatrist, she began to change her mind. Once, just after he'd been confined to a wheelchair—he wouldn't walk—the doctor had come in for the first time, introduced himself, and started chatting. While the doctor was in the middle of his third sentence—something like, "The view isn't bad from . . . "—Jack Potter interrupted. He said, "What are you talking about?"

The doctor said, "Actually, I'll be visiting you like this once a week. I'm treating your depression."

Margie's father said, "I'm not depressed. I'm happy."

The doctor said, "You're happy with merely existing?"

"That's correct."

"The war, Mr. Potter, changed your definition of happiness."

Jack Potter went back to his newspaper and ignored the man. The doctor had been like an oracle to Margie. He was right. Her father was depressed. But he refused to be treated.

Now Margie stood next to his bed in his room, without a book in her hands, and said, "Aunt Jane told me you're coming to this party."

He said, "Yes, I am."

She said, "You don't have to feel that you're expected."

"I know I'm not expected. I'm coming because you'll need me." He didn't say that to the wall, he said it to Margie. His eyes were gray. So were hers. The rest of Margie, supposedly, was her mother.

Margie said, "Thanks, Dad."

She thought: Talk about sacrifices, Martha, my girl. He loves me so much even if he is depressed. He didn't kill himself entirely just on the chance that I might need him—his interpretation of need, not yours, Martha. When Margie drove off from the veterans' home, she wished Martha could only know that he loved her, too. When she was small, Margie would bring her to visit and he'd laugh at her baby nonsense. Once he said to Margie, "Your mother used to write so many letters, Margie. She'd tell me how you reminded her of a drunken sailor—babbling and tumbling all over the place. Now I see what she meant." His eyes were harkening back. For a moment he had a wife again. For a moment he remembered life before he'd been imprisoned. Margie broke the spell, though. She said, "Letters?" His old eyes came back.

"I'm sorry, Margie. I lost them."

"They were lost?"

"No. I lost them."

Margie felt her heart sink.

Jack Potter had, in fact, taught Martha to read. When she was older, she'd come with her mother to visit him once in a while when she was in the mood to sit and read, which wasn't often because she was always so busy. But then she came to feel that life was cheating her out of something—having a normal grandfather. Martha's other grandfather, Denny O'Neill, had died before she was old enough to remember him. Now there was abnormal. Be grateful you were cheated out of him, Margie thought as she drove home.

Clayton T. Bart was in uniform. He had a lot of ribbons, the ones everyone's heard of, and then some others: The Air Force Commendation Medal, the Air Force Achievement Medal, and the Combat Crew Award. Chick had filled him in on more than just Margie; the first thing he did when he walked into Margie's living room was salute Jack Potter sitting in his wheelchair in the corner. Margie's father returned the salute. Then the captain shook Margie's hand, and said, "Pleased to meet you, ma'am." He was very uneasy.

So Margie said, "Want to see my scar?" She was smirking when she said it to put him at his ease. He went to say something, but instead his body began to shake. Margie put her arms around him and he hugged her hard and just broke down. He tried to apologize for losing his composure, and that was what made everyone else at the party cry, too, especially Charlie's family, since they had those Italian genes where emotions came out in a flood, but only on special occasions.

So out came all the food, too, and the bottles and bottles of wine, and everybody started digging in because people can really eat voraciously when in an emotional crisis. That's what Martha told Little Pete's smallest children, who didn't understand what the party was all about and how people could go from happy to sad to happy so fast. Captain Bart didn't really start to talk until they were on the cannoli and the coffee. Oh, to be a worm in a cannoli, Margie said to herself. They sipped their coffee and listened while Charlie took notes off in the corner like he was a monk chronicling some event in the Middle Ages. Before, Margie had said to Charlie, "No tapes." And Charlie said, "But I need to capture this." And then he had looked at Margie's set face and said, "Okay, honey."

Captain Bart poured out every detail of July 6, 1944. But they were the usual details: the wild animals; the apparition-like moment of the Wallendas' appearance; the fire; the panic to get out. He said he grabbed two kids around their waists, tucked each one under his arm like they were footballs, and crawled out under the tent. Captain Bart was from Arkansas, where they were used to tents. City folk aren't, so the citizens of Hartford headed for the entrance they'd come in, no matter that it was blocked by iron bars. That you could go under the walls of a tent had never occurred to them.

He told them that the brigade passing the bodies from over the chute to the blankets laid out on the grass lasted just a minute or so—just a dozen or so children were all that Hermes Wallenda could manage to pull up and over the chute before the heat forced him back. Charlie would have given plenty for Hermes Wallenda's testimony but Margie could well imagine why the youngest Wallenda had refused. The last thing he must have seen before he jumped down off the chute would have been the choking mothers holding their children up to him. All the witnesses from inside the tent said there was no smoke. They could see it all just like they were watching a movie. The smoke didn't come until everyone was either out or forsaken.

Captain Bart had stood on the ground on the other side of the chute and caught the children Hermes Wallenda dropped down to him and then passed them on to an army private behind him. He said a big surge of heat suddenly came through the bars, pushing at him like a great invisible burning hand. Then Hermes Wallenda jumped down and faced him, their eyes inches apart. Captain Bart said that it was the same as looking into hell. "I saw hell in his eyes," he said. The twang was almost entirely gone, not quite, but his Bible-thumping roots lingered. Then they ran, Captain Bart off to see where he could be of more help, Hermes Wallenda to his trailer.

Captain Bart paused for just a second before he said, "Thank God for that wall of heat, though. There is just no question in my mind that those people up against the chute died in an instant." He knew that was what must have happened because even though no fire touched him, his uniform had been burned black, and the hair of his arms was singed off. He'd been leaning against the chute, and when he took off his pants that night there were the beet red imprints of the vertical bars against his thighs. Margie looked over at Chick. Little Miss 1565 had been barely touched by the hand of heat Captain Bart spoke of; she had been protected from it by the crazed people climbing on top of her, fatally crushing her. Captain Bart looked at Margie sitting next to him and said, "You were just a tiny baby. A piece of burning canvas must have fallen on your back. I remember. . . . "

Then he started crying again. Jack Potter from his wheelchair said to him, "Now, son, you just take it easy. Everything's fine now." Martha caught Margie's eye.

Captain Bart, a career air force officer but still a farm boy from the Bible Belt, wiped his nose on his immaculate khaki sleeve and said, "Thank you, sir. I thought . . . the baby . . . " He raised his hands, palms up, and looked at them, and then at Margie. He said, "I thought you were dead."

Jack Potter said, "No, son, she was unconscious."

Margie put down her coffee cup. "Well wouldn't you know it wasn't one of those famous Wallendas who'd left a thumbprint in my back? Just some kid from Arkansas." Margie smiled at him.

She saw Charlie roll his eyes.

Captain Bart managed a smile back at her. She said, "You know, Captain, the thing you have to tell yourself is that I don't remember any of it. It's like you're telling me a story of someone else." What she always said.

Her father said, "That's true, Captain."

Then Jack Potter went back to sipping his coffee. He'd pulled himself out of wherever he was to keep an eye out for Margie, the way he'd always done until she met Charlie. Jack Potter's devotion to his daughter allowed him to be where he wanted to be—nowhere—while he waited to get back to his wife. Before the war. At the party, his words, "That's true, Captain," were the last he spoke for the rest of the day.

Martha said to her mother later, "I'm sorry, but I just can't help but wonder what he was feeling when he dropped napalm on all those other babies."

Margie said, "God help him."

Martha said, "Right."

Sometimes, Margie just wanted to smack her, just the way kids her age wanted to smack the world.

The day after the party, Margie took a ride back to Charter Oak Terrace. Seeing her Aunt Jane and Big Pete and Little Pete together with her father made her want to reach back to another time, when she was a little girl, before anything began to seem terribly wrong. Just the way her father wanted to reach back to some time before the war but couldn't. She knew the cherry tree wouldn't be there anymore after so many years, and it wasn't. There was a washing machine under the window instead. A new one. The Puerto Ricans put it outside because there was no room inside, same way they did back in San Juan. They didn't know about water lines freezing in the winter yet. Someone would tell them, and they'd make a place for it. She asked the Puerto Rican family who lived in her old apartment if she could come in and see where she had been raised till she was six years old. The Puerto Rican family agreed immediately because they had a strong empathy for homesickness.

Margie was absolutely appalled at the thought that a father and a child, let alone a huge Puerto Rican family could live in such a small space. Downstairs, a minuscule kitchen butted up against a tiny living room, and upstairs there were two bedrooms with barely enough space for a bed and a bureau each, and a bathroom. The rooms were filled with furniture—mostly cots—and kids. There were curtains dividing the bedrooms and the living room, too, so that there were three extra bedrooms. But the clearest memory Margie had brought with her was of the coal furnace in a little alcove by the back door. She remembered watching her father shovel coal into the red insides. And Margie remembered what she'd been thinking then; she'd watch her father and try to imagine what the circus fire had been like. When she was little— when no one would speak to her of it. But she'd heard the whispers and began to put it together with why she had no mother.

Now there was an oil burner, and next to it, an oval basket lined with a pink-checked blanket holding a sleeping baby. Things began to melt down for Margie when she saw the little baby so close to the oil burner with fire hidden somewhere inside it in the same place where that big black coal

furnace used to be. Margie heard herself mumbling something to the Puerto Ricans, saying good-bye and thanking
them, and then getting out of there so she could breathe
again. And once outside in her car, she heard the question
she'd heard over and over again that would turn her father to
steel: "How could she have taken such a tiny baby to the circus?"

Puerto Ricans take their babies everywhere, even to circus-
es. They put them to sleep next to the oil burner. How can
you put a baby to sleep next to an oil burner? Because it's
warm there, and the motor has a nice hum and besides, there
isn't any room for her anywhere else. Margie hadn't asked
them the question she hoped no one else would ever ask, and
they didn't ask her about her mother. In the car, later, she
smelled a sweet fragrance. She was holding a half-empty
plastic cup of *tamarinda* juice the Puerto Ricans must have
given her. The juice helped her to gain control so that she
wouldn't crack up her new Seville. Also, to help herself gain
control, she thought about the complicated plot of a book
she'd read recently, *The Tamarind Seed*. She thought: They
don't make thrillers like that one anymore. With irony. She
would go home and recommend it to Martha.

But the image of Martha that came to her just then was of
Martha in her crib. An infant like the baby in the basket,
maybe six months old. Margie saw herself lifting a hungry,
squalling Martha from her crib. She watched herself go downstairs to the living room and sit on the sofa to breast-feed the
baby while she got back to the book she was almost finished
with. But Martha distracted her from the book. Six months is
a comical age. Since babies begin sitting up at that stage, they
gain a new perspective on life. Margie would prop her in a
high chair and Martha would eat cubes of bananas or pieces of
ziti. She especially loved to pick up a big steak bone and chew
on it. Margie thought that all her chewing probably soothed
her aching gums. But mostly, Martha loved Cheerios. She had

such long, fine fingers, and Margie loved watching her pick up a single Cheerios between finger and thumb and bring it slowly to her mouth, watching it the whole time until her eyes crossed. Then she'd push it into her mouth and while she gummed it around she'd stare at her empty finger and thumb and Margie would say, "Martha, you ate it." Her voice would distract the baby, and Martha would give her a big smile and move on to the next Cheerios. Eating as a concept, Margie could see, was yet to be fathomed.

The day Margie was remembering became clearer. Martha was sucking away at her mother's breast, and once the initial hunger pangs were assuaged, she then peeked up at Margie. She smiled and Margie's nipple slipped out of her mouth. Martha pulled her head back and looked at it, and then her gaze drifted back up to Margie, and then back to the nipple. Up came Martha's hand and she caught Margie's nipple between her thumb and finger and pulled it into her mouth, looking into her mother's eyes all the while. She repeated this procedure several times, and then Margie couldn't help but smile; one of her body parts was being treated like Cheerios. She said, "Martha, you silly goose." But Martha was serious. There was an expression of wonder that had come over her as she realized that not only did her mother always hold her and keep her cozy when she ate, it was her mother she was eating.

When she dozed off, Margie lay her on a blanket on the sofa beside her. And Margie knew that if she walked out of Martha's life right then, when she was six months old, Martha would suffer a horrible loss. Of course, she'd at least have a daddy to hug and hold her. Margie hadn't had that. Her daddy had been a prisoner of war. Whatever that meant. Margie didn't know as he would never speak of it.

Margie cried and cried. She was not the crying type. So she didn't know how to stop. All she could think of was that poor, poor baby, burned so badly, in such pain, and without her mother to help her. Deserted by her mother was what it must have certainly felt like. To associate Martha with utter despair was impossible for Margie. But that was what it must have been. The hard thing was not talking to Charlie about this. He'd get crazed, and he was crazed enough, bound and determined to figure out who set that fire.

Now she steered the Seville into a U-turn, and Margie headed away from Charter Oak Terrace to her Aunt Jane's house. She sped along, thinking she had mourned her mother after all. She had grieved in some terrible baby way and she wanted to find out about it. She thought: My Aunt Jane who had a baby of her own to take care of stepped in and raised me while I must have been in one wretched state. Margie had always shown her aunt appreciation—buying her special presents and inviting her places—but she had never really come out and thanked her. She'd never thought to. And not only that, she wanted to find out exactly what else there was to thank her for.

She pulled into her aunt's driveway, ran up the walk, and rang the bell. Her aunt opened the door and Margie said, "I came to thank you for raising me and helping my father when he came home." Her aunt got her into the house and said, "Now you just calm yourself, Margie. You know your happiness has always been thanks enough."

Over coffee, Margie did calm down. She asked, "What was I like, Aunt Jane, when I was a baby? After my mother died."

Jane said, "Well, you were very, very sick."

Margie didn't let her stop there. She said, "Was I in a lot of physical pain?" hoping she was so that she wouldn't picture herself as a baby like Martha, wondering why her mother wouldn't come to her. Aunt Jane told Margie that the doctors at Hartford Hospital had seen to it that she had a lot morphine. She told her that the hospital had been just two years old and by some miracle was chosen as the site of an experimental burn unit exclusively designed for a civilian disaster—

in case the Jerries bombed New York the way the Japs had Pearl Harbor. And since the doctors at Pearl Harbor had learned that there was no substitute for blood plasma in treating burn patients, Hartford Hospital had had gallons of frozen blood plasma. Jane said, "You know, Margie, it was a gift from God that Hartford Hospital was five minutes away from the circus. We'd have lost a thousand people, if not. We'd have lost you."

"How did I act?"

"What?"

"I mean, how was I? Besides the pain."

At first, her aunt didn't speak. But then she forced herself back because she could see Margie needed her to. "Even with the morphine, you were constantly looking for your mother. When you started to get some of your strength back, you would search. With just your eyes. You'd try not to fall asleep so you could find her. Every time the door to your hospital room opened, you'd get all alert and at first, smile. Then when it wasn't your mother, you'd cry. All over again." Margie's aunt picked up her napkin and blew her nose. "It got so that the nurses would call out who they were before they'd come into your room."

Jane went on to say that, fortunately for her, Little Pete was a very outgoing baby and loved to have other people take care of him, so she'd leave him with different neighbors so she could spend a lot of time in the hospital with her best buddy's daughter.

Then she said, "It took about three months."

Margie said, "Three months?"

"Before you stopped looking for your mother." She sighed. "When your burns were finally healing, you still weren't getting better. I mean, you acted sick. So I asked the doctor to please let me take you home and he said it would be okay." Now she smiled at Margie. She said, "You were so glad to see Little Pete again. The two of you recognized each other right away. He kept piling all his little toys around you. Giving them to you so you'd stay. He loved you, Little Pete did. Loved you from the first day he saw you. Guess that's why I'm blessed with so many grandchildren."

Margie asked, "How was I after that?"

"After . . . ?"

After I was with you for a while."

"Well, you had become a serious baby. And then you were a serious child. Your father came back and the two of you were the same. It wasn't until you were eleven or twelve years old that you got back that merry disposition you inherited from your mother."

Margie didn't tell her aunt that "merry" had just been adolescent nerves.

"And your father . . . well . . . I guess I haven't seen that man laugh since before he left for overseas."

Margie had a good wit and she made people laugh, but she didn't find many things funny. She had to think about laughing in order to do it. Charlie was the same way. Some people just naturally burst into laughter. That didn't happen to Margie and she'd never seen Charlie do it, either. Martha made up for them. She'd always laughed and giggled and chuckled enough for the three of them. Four. Margie added her father to the list.

When Margie was back in her car, she wondered: Why Charlie? She wondered that because she was feeling bitter about what happened to her. What the hell did Charlie ever lose?

Chapter Nine

That evening, Margie said to Charlie, "My first memory had to do with fire."

He looked up at her from his dinner. He said, "You were too young to remember."

"Not with the circus fire. Another fire."

And Margie lapsed into another tale, all her own this time, describing the recollection to her attentive husband.

It was when she was a small child. She was sitting across from her father at dinner, reading *Casper the Friendly Ghost*. Margie looked up from the comic book and watched him for a few moments. Then she asked, "Daddy, what if I died in the fire, too?"

He glanced over the top of his paper at her, and without taking any time to think, he gave her his answer. Since he answered so quickly Margie knew he'd already asked himself that question too. He said, "I would have committed *suttee*."

Then he put his paper back up between them again. It was a very ugly word he'd said; she didn't know what it meant and felt glad that she didn't know. Margie was too young to read a dictionary so she couldn't find out, but that didn't really matter. What mattered was that he'd given her an answer.

Margie paused from her story and said to Charlie, "You know, that's all children ever want—answers, not necessarily meanings."

"I guess."

"I remember Little Pete's son asking something at the dinner table when we were over there for one of the kids' birthdays. You had to work. Baby Pete asked, 'How does the sperm get to the egg?'"

Charlie smiled. "Kids always wait till they're at the dinner table to ask about the birds and the bees, don't they?"

"They do." Margie smiled, too. "Well, Little Pete took Baby Pete into the living room, broke out the medical encyclopedia, and explained the mechanics. When they came back to the table, they sat down and Baby Pete looked over at Little Pete and asked, 'But, Daddy, how does the sperm *get* to the egg?' So Martha looked down the table and told him, '*Swim*, Baby Pete. They *swim*.'"

Charlie said, "And Baby Pete was happy and went back to his meat loaf."

"Exactly. Charlie, the one-word answer my father gave me—*suttee*—was all I needed. So I went back to *Casper the Friendly Ghost.*

"But that word kept sticking with me until I was old enough to think about meaning. *Suttee* would come back in dreams, or I'd see something in a book at school, or once when I saw a dead, stiff cat on the road."

"What—"

"And about that time, Charlie, I had a big rubber ball,

almost the size of a basketball; it had red and white stripes around the middle, and white stars on blue everywhere else. One day, it was run over by the bread truck. The ball got cut into six or seven pieces. Kids played with the pieces and kept them, and passed them around. Every so often, months later—and months is a long time to a kid—I'd be in the car and we'd pass by a strange kid I didn't know playing with a piece of my ball, and terrible images of dead, stiff cats, and nightmares, and the word *suttee* would come into my head."

Charlie didn't try to interrupt, to find out what *suttee* meant. Instead, he listened to Margie's story, waiting for the denouement that would eventually come.

"The older I got, the more curious I became about the word and about my father, too, as a matter of fact. I wondered more and more about what he'd told me, the thing he'd have done if I'd died in the fire. Whatever it was must have been more shocking than suicide to have such an ugly name. He would have committed that other thing—the strange *suttee* thing.

"Then when I was around seven, I asked my Aunt Jane what *suttee* meant. She told me she'd never heard of a *suttee*. Dictionaries aren't exactly in my aunt's frame of reference. After that, when I realized that even Aunt Jane didn't know what my father was talking about—that it most definitely must have meant something even worse than suicide—the word went away for a long while." Margie looked over at Charlie from the window where she'd been gazing. "Or as Martha would say, I suppressed it.

"Then when I was around ten, I spotted the word in the newspaper."

Margie's father read two newspapers every day: The *Hartford Courant* in the morning, and in the evening, the *New York Times*, which arrived in the mail. She came to be a newspaper reader herself, what with that influence. She loved both those newspapers, too, the *Courant* because she learned all about her home, and the *New York Times* because it was an international newspaper and she was curious about what was going on in the world.

"You know what Martha told me one time, Charlie?"

"What, honey?"

"She said I treat the articles in the *Times* like my novels. Good stories, but make-believe."

"Was she right?"

"Well, it's no fun to imagine that the perils of the world are real perils." He didn't say anything, "Anyway, every day, I'd come home from school and get the mail, which was bills and the *New York Times*. First I'd go to the bathroom, then change into my play clothes, and I'd get some cookies and sit at the kitchen table with the newspaper. I'd say I was a fifth-grader when the front page of the *Times* had this picture of a funeral pyre in India. A dead man's body was burning—his body was a long lump but you could see his face. His widow had just hurled herself across him. Her hair was on fire. The article was about a humanitarian group exposing the rite of *suttee,* saying that the widow didn't volunteer to die out of love. She'd been drugged and tossed onto the fire so that the man's family wouldn't be financially responsible for her."

Charlie's eyes were narrower.

"My father meant to volunteer, Charlie. Out of love. And I was a little girl, so I didn't realize he'd been speaking, um, metaphorically. I thought he would have lit a bonfire on her grave and mine, and lay down on it."

"I'm sorry, Margie." Charlie covered her hand with his.

"So then I got up from the table and went out, and buried the newspaper in the backyard. That night, my father came home from work with cream puffs from the bakery for our dessert. My father fried lamb chops. When the lamb chops were cooked, we read and ate. I read my comic books at dinner instead of my books in case I spilled anything."

By the time Margie was nine she had had a stack of several

hundred comic books in a box on the floor of her closet. She'd read the new one her father bought her on Saturday night, and then she'd put it face down in a pile next to the box. When the box was empty, she'd turn the other pile over and put it in the box, and start reading from the top again. Margie looked forward most to *Uncle Scrooge*, *Casper*, *Blackhawk*, and a one-time issue of *Cinderella*. Every time she got to *Cinderella* it was a victory that her father hadn't married a wicked stepmother. And she looked forward to finding out who Prince Charming would be, never thinking for a minute that because there wasn't a wicked stepmother in her life there might not be a Prince Charming, either. But of course, there was. He was holding her hand right now.

"So he read and ate while I waited, making believe I was engrossed. I tried to eat my cream puff, but I kept gagging. Then he folded up the paper, the *Courant*, and he said, 'Where's the *Times*, Margie?'

"I lied. I told him it hadn't come."

Charlie rubbed the back of her wrist. "Poor kid."

"Yeah."

"Want some coffee? I'll grind some special."

"Thanks, Charlie."

While Charlie puttered, Margie thought about the rest. Her lie hadn't been a hard one to say because sometimes the *Times* wouldn't come, and then they'd get two the next day in the mail. After the lie, her father sighed, got up, and went and found the book he was reading. The next evening, Margie realized how her father's daily habits sustained him. When yesterday's *Times* still hadn't come it was as if a drug had been withdrawn. He was unable to read the new one without reading the old one. Obsessive. Not romantically obsessive—neurotically. "Compulsive," Martha once explained. "Like Lady Macbeth. Like Dad."

Jack Potter paced around after dinner and then said, "I'm going to take a walk to the library, Margie."

She said, "Okay. I'll be in my room." She knew he'd read the missing *Times* at the library.

He had come home very late. She heard him stumble. Two doors down from the library was the Brookside Tavern. Her father went there on the anniversary of the circus fire and on her mother's birthday. He just couldn't concentrate on reading on those days. The next day he'd be fine, though. He'd take aspirins with his orange juice before heading off to Fuller Brush.

Margie had been consumed by pity for her father. She tended to feel sorry for him all the time, but she had been desolate on that night. She lay awake listening to the stumbling. She had prayed for him. The she had set her alarm early and gone downstairs and set the table and put two aspirin next to his glass, her offering as a way of apologizing. They had sat down and he'd taken them. He hadn't said anything. The relief they'd felt that neither spoke was enormous. And oh, what Martha would have to say about that, Margie thought.

Charlie sat back down while the coffee dripped through the filter.

"People always felt so sorry for me, Charlie. But I'd tell them not to bother. I'd keep telling them I was just a baby when my mother died like I told Captain Bart. Like I've always told you. I couldn't have really missed her. And growing up without a mother wasn't so bad since I had no idea what it was like to have one—I had nothing to compare not having a mother with. Sort of like asking a twin what it's like to be a twin.

"My father took good care of me. When I felt envy toward my friends and my cousins because they had mothers and I didn't, I felt so disloyal."

"I know."

They drank their coffee. He always said that to Margie. I know. But he didn't know. He didn't know about the day on the sofa with baby Martha and the bubbles of resentment, and how more and more sprang up every day.

Chapter Ten

In all the years she was married to Charlie, Margie had liked to think that something momentous would happen. Captain Bart's visit wasn't as momentous to her as it was to her family, but she finally came to realize that his appearance was as momentous as things were going to get. She realized that the night she told Charlie about her first fire memory, *suttee*. She continued to humor Charlie, though, while she figured out how she might go about not humoring him without hurting him. How do you betray a person gently? And then, right when she was in the middle of her frustration, something momentous did happen, in the persona of a Bob Corcoran, who arrived at the front door unexpectedly.

He was a man around Charlie's age who had been to the circus. He had escaped the flames unhurt. Physically unhurt. He'd flown in from his home in Seattle, a home that was about as far away as he could get from Hartford, Connecticut. Margie took to him right away because he had an earnest look about him, the kind Charlie had had when she'd met him. The kind of earnestness Charlie had had when he'd asked her where her scars came from and she thought he was asking her where she'd gotten *To Kill a Mockingbird*. But that look was gone from Charlie now. With each passing year, Charlie's look had become less earnest and more flinty. More a fireman's look than a searcher's. Margie felt alienated from that look, but Charlie didn't notice because she hid her alienation from him behind a book.

After Bob Corcoran had answered Charlie's initial questions, Charlie didn't ask any more. He didn't have to. Corcoran was a gusher, and he didn't start with happy memories like most did. None of that nervous hesitation in describing how exciting it was to be going to the circus. He didn't speak of the heat of the day mixed with the thrill. The nervousness that was absent in him had always been immediately obvious in the other witnesses; it arose from the guilt they felt about their anticipation. With great pain and struggle they'd try to smile and they'd say: "I couldn't wait for the circus to start . . . couldn't wait."

Bob Corcoran placed himself on the Map—in the deadly area of Grandstand A, just a few yards from the main entrance, with the chute running between. Then he said that his eight-year-old sister and four-year-old brother had been killed by the circus fire. That was how he put it. They were killed "*by* the fire." Charlie took note. Corcoran went on to say that his mother had been taken to the hospital, but her face was so badly burned that she couldn't talk. "Which," he said, "was why there was all that confusion about my sister." Then he stopped, and then he whispered a name. "Louise."

"What confusion was that?" Charlie asked him.

Bob Corcoran said, "Louise was Little Miss 1565."

Charlie's eyes flickered over to Margie and back to Corcoran. Margie made sure the tape recorder was still going around and the reel wasn't about to run out.

Charlie said, "My uncle would be very interested in hearing what you have to say. He—"

"I *spoke* to your uncle." An anger rose. He checked it. "After the fire. He didn't believe me. No one did. I was hoping you would. It's taken me all these years to finally realize that someone might believe me. That I'm an adult now— why shouldn't someone believe me, damn it!"

Without skipping a beat, Charlie said, "I believe you." The man looked up at him as if he'd heard an oracle speak. Charlie asked, "Why do you suppose no one believed you?"

A hundred things went through the man's mind all at once. Margie watched his struggle. But all that he could get out was another "Damn it." Charlie said, "Take your time." Corcoran leaned back and settled into the chair as if he were at the dentist's and had finally resolved himself to the fact that he couldn't escape the drill. He'd come too far.

"I saw the picture and I identified her. But my aunt told them I was mistaken. They chose to believe my aunt and not me."

"Your aunt?"

"Yes."

"She survived the fire, too?"

"She wasn't at the fire."

Margie asked, "Can I get you a cup of coffee, Mr. Corcoran?"

He said, "Yes, please. And it's Bob."

The coffee helped all three of them. Puttering and pouring and settling back down softened the tension hanging about, suspended in the air.

Charlie said, "Let's start with the hardest part. Get it over with."

"It was all hard."

Charlie asked, "Then tell me how you survived the fire and how it was that Louise didn't."

Bob Corcoran took a sip of his coffee first and then he began. He never mentioned the animal act or the Wallendas. He skipped that just as he'd skipped his anticipation and happy frame of mind. He went right to the fire. He said, "At first, we just stared at the flame for a few seconds. Everyone did, all at once. The whole sea of faces turned away from the top of the tent to the spot of fire. I think that was because the tent had become so dark—the lights had gone out and the beam of the spotlight made the rest seem darker. Then someone yelled, 'Fire,' but other people said, right away, 'Oh, sit down. They'll have that out in a jiffy.'"

He took another sip, gingerly, as if it were too hot. Margie knew it wasn't. He looked over at the Map. Corcoran said, "In the next moment it was as if the tent was a volcano. It became a live volcano erupting all over us. The tent erupted."

"And then?"

"And then the fire spread faster than your eyes could follow. The heat was so terrible that the ropes caught immediately even though they weren't anywhere near the burning canvas. People started to scream, and get up, and run down the grandstand. We were sitting halfway up. My mother said to me, 'Take your sister and get out of the tent.'

"My mother had my little brother in her arms. The last I saw of them was my mother's back—she had on a flowered dress. A real pretty dress. Timmy's legs were hooked around her waist, and his arms were wrapped around her neck so tight I don't know how she breathed. Timmy was staring over her shoulder at me, but he wasn't seeing me.

"I grabbed Louise and held on to her, but people were pushing us down. Knocking us down. They kept stepping on us. So I figured, let them get by, then we'll climb to the top of the grandstand, jump down, and get out under the tent."

When Bob said that, a glance from Charlie flickered over to Margie. Not a city boy. He knew a circus tent wasn't a concrete wall. But why didn't his mother? She'd headed straight for the entrance, even though it was blocked by an eight-foot-high tunnel made of steel bars.

Bob talked. "By the time we got to the top of the grandstand, the side of the tent was already burned—gone. Sheets of burning canvas were flying all over. None landed on us. The heat hurt you, though. Just the heat. I told Louise we had to jump, but she got scared and wouldn't do it. She just froze. I looked behind me. One of the three poles was starting to come down. The middle pole was swaying. The ropes holding the poles were almost eaten up.

"There was a Negro man directly below us, looking up. He stretched his arms up into the air, up to us, and he shouted, 'Jump, you children, jump!' Louise came out of her shock. She looked down at the man, then at me, and just turned around and ran back down the grandstand. I screamed at her to come back, but she wouldn't. So I closed my eyes and jumped. The Negro man and I fell on top of each other and then he got me up. He said, 'Run, run!' And he shoved me and I ran off."

Bob Corcoran had to put down his coffee, his hands were trembling so. Margie found that she was gritting her teeth.

Charlie said, "Where did you run to?"

"I just ran. But right away I found a cop—there were lots of cops coming—and I told him my mother and my brother and sister were in there. The cop told me not to worry, that he'd find them. And then another cop took me to a truck that was shuttling children down Barbour Street to a church. It was a tobacco wagon. It was full of stalks of tobacco leaves. The police had commandeered it. I climbed in with all the other kids but Louise and Timmy weren't there."

Now it was time for Charlie to divert the witness, no matter that he might be the brother of the Little Miss. To stop him in his tracks to learn what small thing Bob Corcoran might have seen that he'd never thought about. He asked, "Bob, was your father overseas at this time?"

"I don't know."

"You don't know?" For once, it was Charlie who was diverted.

"That's right. I didn't have any idea where my father was. Still don't. He left when my mother was pregnant with Timmy. My aunt took us kids in, but she didn't take my mother in because my mother didn't want any more of her charity—she was just relieved that her kids would have a nice place. My aunt lived in Simsbury—on farmland. She was my mother's sister. She and her husband had no children. My mother stayed in Hartford and worked to support herself. She was a cleaning woman at the Aetna. We spent one weekend a month with her. The lady she shared her apartment with would go visiting relatives on that weekend. The apartment had one room.

"On Fourth of July weekend, we got to stay with her a few days extra. She'd saved up for four circus tickets."

Then Bob stopped. It wasn't a pause, it was a stop. Margie had been wondering just what thing would make him stop. It was the memory of happiness. His last happiness, she knew. Behind the earnestness was despair. She recognized it. Margie may not have remembered the despair she'd felt as a baby, but the fact that she'd experienced it so terribly allowed her to see it clearly in him. And Charlie, of course, could look like that sometimes.

Charlie said, "What happened next?"

"Nothing."

Margie's throat caught. Charlie said, "Did you see anyone set the fire?"

She couldn't believe her ears. Charlie had never come right out and asked that question directly. She got goose bumps. What was this? Did Charlie think this man set it? Little Miss

1565's brother? Bob said, "No one set it. It was some kind of natural combustion because of the heat."

He said this with such authority that Margie could understand how taken aback Charlie was. Just for a moment, though. Charlie said, "How do you know that?"

"I'm an engineer. The spot of flame everyone talks about was not just one spot of flame. It was the biggest of several and so, drew your eye. But bits of tiny fires were being created in several places, and then they all came together. Because of the high heat of the day. Because the canvas was coated with paraffin and gasoline. Because of the breeze. Like a farmer's barn that just lights up on a summer night because the hay's so dry. Spontaneous combustion."

And then Bob refused to say anything more on the subject, no matter that Charlie prodded. Dead issue. He saw things in terms of dead issues, but at least, now he had found the stamina to come back to Hartford and give his sister peace. The rest of the recording was her story: who she was, how old she was, the way she looked, and the bizarre set of circumstances that kept her identity secret. After he left, Charlie called Chick. Charlie said, "Uncle Chick. A fellow just left. He's Little Miss 1565's brother. Come hear the tape."

While they waited for Chick, Margie asked Charlie if Bob could have been right about how the fire started. Charlie said no, he couldn't be. "He was believing what he wanted to believe. Fellow can't handle someone deliberately wiping out his whole family. Who could? I know you can't, Margie.

"He was right about a farmer's barn, though. The piles of hay in the loft, under a baking sun, become compost—bacterial debris in the center keeps heating up until it finally combusts. The core of the pile bursts into flame. But it can't happen in a circus tent. People aren't bacterial debris.

"And he was right about that ring of fire everyone mentions. It was the first of many, lit by flying embers from the little bonfire the arsonist had set at the bottom of the tent, outside. Outside, behind Grandstand A."

Margie said, "At first, Charlie, did you think he was the one who set it?"

Charlie looked away. "I thought I heard something there. . . ."

And then Chick came through the front door like he was being chased by a pack of wild dogs. Breathless. Speechless. Didn't shut the door behind him. Margie said, "Want a glass of wine first?"

He gasped words at her as he rushed past to the war room, "I want to hear this."

They followed him in. He collapsed into a chair, the one Bob Corcoran had been sitting in. Margie turned the knob on the tape recorder. She and Charlie sat together and listened again with Chick, as Charlie took Bob through the rest of his story. The rest of his story held no business interest to Charlie, only human interest. Margie found Bob even more mesmerizing the second time around, her shock out of the way, replaced by clear images, like in a good book when you read it the second time.

Bob said, "The police took me to my aunt and uncle, who were at a station house. They were so glad to see me. At first. But then, they wanted me to tell them where Timmy and Louise were. I didn't know. My aunt became hysterical so a cop drove us—my aunt and me—back home while my uncle went to the armory. That's where the bodies were. He wanted to do that first. Only when he was positive they weren't dead would he go to Hartford Hospital. He was gone till the next morning. My aunt stayed up in the kitchen all night, smoking. I was with her when he came home. He said, 'Timmy died an hour ago.' And my aunt screamed, 'But not Louise! Not Louise!' A doctor had to come to our house to give her a shot."

There was a click and a pause, and scratching. Chick

looked up from the tape recorder. He'd been staring at it. He said, "What happened?"

Charlie said, "He broke down. Margie cut the tape till he could talk again."

Bob Corcoran's voice returned. "Louise was my aunt's favorite. She always tied ribbons in her hair and dressed her in lacy clothes, even for school. So my uncle told my aunt that some family had found Louise—they were taking care of her while they tried to find out who she belonged to. My aunt was so relieved. I watched her. She kept saying, 'Yes, yes. Some other family had her for the night.' She never mentioned Timmy. Or my mother. Now, I would guess, my uncle saw Louise's body at the hospital, but didn't identify her. He worshiped my aunt. He couldn't give her children. And so he wouldn't take away the one she favored.

"A couple days later a policeman came with a picture of Louise's face. He apologized first. Told my uncle and me that the little girl in the picture was dead. I said it was my sister, and my uncle kept saying I was mistaken because I was just a child and I was so upset. He told them it was definitely not Louise. He wouldn't let them show the picture to my aunt. He kept telling them she was too distraught and that she was under sedation besides. Then he sent me to my room. That's when he must have told the cop that he'd found Louise, and probably that she was dead. He'd buried Timmy. He must have said he buried Louise, too—that the girl in the picture was someone else.

"For weeks, my aunt repeated the same thing over and over again: The other family was taking good care of Louise. She'd go on and on about how the people were probably from out of town and were having trouble finding us. That they were a well-to-do family who knew what was best for children. So after a while—I guess after I couldn't take it anymore—I started to think that maybe I was wrong. Maybe I'd made a mistake. And, of course, I did want to believe that

Louise was alive. My mother had told me to get her out—to save her. But I didn't. Maybe someone else . . . " At this point Bob Corcoran put his head in his hands. Margie thought she saw mist in Charlie's eyes. When the man looked up again, he said, "We moved to Massachusetts. Then we moved again, to Maine. Far away."

Charlie asked him, "But what about your mother?"

Bob said, "She died in the hospital, too. I didn't want to be the only one left. I wanted my sister to be alive, too."

"Did you ever get to visit with your mother before she died?"

Bob said, "No, I didn't."

A loud voice from out of nowhere boomed, "Turn it off."

That was Chick. Margie had never heard that tone from him. Charlie said, "Jesus. You sounded just like my father. What's the matter?"

"Rhoda Banks."

Charlie waited. And then Chick told his story in a voice that was just like Bob Corcoran's—cracking and shaking. He started with, "Corcoran's mother didn't die. His mother survived the fire."

Charlie said, "How about taping this, Margie."

Margie put on a new tape. Chick told them that Bob Corcoran's mother and his brother Timmy had been found alive, just like Little Miss 1565, at the bottom of the pile of bodies up against the animal chute. Margie thought, Louise did find them. Mother and son had been fused together by their burned flesh. They were taken to the hospital that way, given shots of morphine, and separated by a surgeon.

"Surgeon told me he didn't believe either of them would live. The boy died a few hours later." He closed his eyes for a few seconds. He said, "Bob Corcoran's mother, Rhoda Banks, was in the hospital for eight months, her face so badly injured that her lips couldn't move. Her eyes were bandaged.

"When she gained enough strength—this is months

later—she wrote on a piece of paper that a Mr. and Mrs. John Corcoran of Simsbury were her closest relatives. I checked the records and told the nurses to tell her that her younger two children had died. If one of the men reported that the Corcoran boy identified his sister as the Little Miss, the guy never said anything. Uncle must have been pretty convincing. Jesus."

Charlie and Margie watched Chick wipe his forehead with his handkerchief. "I'll tell ya, I felt bad for that woman. Anyway, we couldn't find the Corcorans. They'd moved. The nurses went bullshit, but there was no way we would have followed those people up. We kept trying to find them, but it turned out, they'd moved again. To Maine. No forwarding address. I expressed my apologies to Mrs. Banks, told her we'd keep looking. We did. Nothing.

"Then, about a year later, she called me. Rhoda Banks told me her brother-in-law reached her and that he told her the surviving son eventually died of complications from his injuries."

"What?" Margie couldn't help herself.

"Let him finish, honey."

"But why would he say such a thing?"

Chick said, "Yeah. Why? It never crossed my mind that it was a lie. Who would have thought to question that Corcoran guy—we only worked with the squeaky wheels. Hundred and fifty dead kids needing to be sorted out. Why should we question him? His story was simple."

Chick, Margie knew, was really asking himself how he had messed up. But what was he supposed to do? Keep going back to people and asking if they'd counted correctly? Are you sure you lost two kids? Maybe you lost three. Are you sure this little girl isn't your little girl? And then the Corcorans were just an aunt and an uncle, not parents. Margie saw that Chick, everybody actually, would rather have kept the Little Miss a mystery rather than have another heartbroken family; there had been so many.

Chick got up and stood still for just a few seconds, and then he got on the phone for half an hour. Margie and Charlie listened as he put the wheels into motion. His network of friends and comrades tracked down Rhoda Banks. She was at St. Theresa's Nursing Home in West Hartford. She was indigent. Chick went off to Bob Corcoran's hotel to tell him that his mother was not dead, to apologize, and then to bring him to see his mother. Charlie and Margie met them at the nursing home. Margie refused to let Charlie bring the tape recorder. "Not now, Charlie. If anybody says something worth remembering, you'll remember it." He wanted to protest, but it was Margie who was asking for something so he didn't.

Mrs. Banks screamed when Bob came into the room, even though she knew he was coming—the nuns had prepared her. But in that first instant, she thought Bob was her husband. It took a while to calm her. Then she was so overwhelmed with guilt for not knowing Bob was alive, and Bob was so enraged at his aunt and uncle's deception, that Mrs. Banks started weeping terribly and Bob began punching one hand into the other as if he were a robot with his dial set to that one action. The nuns kept trying to soothe Mrs. Banks but no one had the courage to reach out to her son. And then Chick, though he tried, could not contain himself. Amidst the wailing his voice boomed the way it had in the war room, his question a clap of thunder, and they were all struck by it. "*Why didn't you identify your daughter, Mrs. Banks?*"

It took a while to set in. At some point, after she could speak, obviously Rhoda Banks must have been shown the picture. She must have seen it in the papers. It was there every year, year after year, in the Hartford *Courant* and a thousand other papers across the country.

The nuns gaped at Chick. Bob stopped pounding at himself, and Mrs. Banks turned to stone. She made a little noise and they all looked at her. Margie knew about scars. The ones on Mrs. Banks's face were terrible. And she looked like such an old, old woman, though she was several years younger than Chick. Chick said in his normal voice, "Please, Mrs. Banks."

Rhoda Banks said, "My sister wanted to believe her alive. Well, so did I. And my brother-in-law . . . maybe . . ." she stopped, took a breath, and now her voice came out angry. ". . . he must have figured . . . he knew that maybe . . . if his wife at least had Bobby . . ."

Then she covered her ravaged face with her hands. Bob Corcoran said, "He figured if she had me, she would forget about Louise. Well, she didn't."

He went over to his mother, and took her hands down, and held them tight. His mother looked into his eyes. And then Mrs. Banks said to him, mother to son, "What did Louise call your Aunt Elizabeth?"

Bob pressed his lips together, but he got the word out: "Mama."

Mrs. Banks said to Chick, "Louise called my sister Mama. After living with my sister, she called her Mama and she didn't call me anything. She was my sister's daughter. My sister took her from me." Her eyes went back to Bob. "But why did she have to take you, too? My big boy?" And she pulled Bob's hands back to her cheeks. Her voice came through the fingers of Bob's hands, and everyone listened, paralyzed. "I wanted to be dead. Sometimes I just thought—even years after the fire—well, we're all dead. Then I'd remember. I wasn't. Later . . . in the papers . . . I saw the picture. But Louise had straight hair, not curly hair. When I saw the picture . . . after all that time . . . the pretty curls . . . I couldn't be sure, could I? My sister . . . my sister had Louise's hair styled and permed. And I . . . I had to cut my own hair with my sewing scissors." She was drifting, but she came right back. "It was the curls. My daughter had straight hair, not curls. That's what I kept thinking about. And . . . and maybe Louise was alive, after all. Maybe two little girls got mixed up. . . . Maybe one of my children had lived. . . ." She drifted.

Then Bob said, "Mama. One of them did."

The old woman's head turned back to her son. And then she became overwhelmed and began weeping. Weeping and weeping. Bob held her in his arms, kept saying he was going to bring her home with him and take care of her. Margie broke down. Charlie put his arm around her. Chick had his head in his hands. The nuns didn't cry; instead they prayed furiously, their lips moving a mile a minute. Their prayers worked. It took a while, but a wave of calm spread across the room. The crying became sniffling and the nuns passed around a box of Kleenex. And finally, someone spoke again. Rhoda Banks. She said to Bob, "You're a fine man. You're a handsome man, like your Pop." And that got him going again. He couldn't control his tears, but they weren't tears of despair, or rage either, like at first. They were tears of relief. Tears of peace.

"It was the Depression, Bobby. He had to go find work. But I guess he couldn't. He knew your aunt would take care of us. Her husband had money. That's why he didn't come back. For our own good."

Margie could hear her heart beating. She was no longer feeling pity for Bob Corcoran, but envy. He had found his mother.

Bob Corcoran's whole body was shaking, and Rhoda Banks did her best to hold him and pat him. But still it wasn't over. Chick cleared his throat, Margie guessed to keep himself from bellowing again. He asked, "Mrs. Banks, could you positively identify the photograph of Little Miss 1565 as your daughter, Louise Corcoran, today?"

Bob said, "Banks. Louise Banks. My uncle changed my name . . . after."

Chick said, "Louise Banks."

Rhoda Banks said, "No, I couldn't."

But Charlie, who loved his own little baby girl so and whose mind worked in different ways from the rest, said, "Do you have a picture of Louise, Mrs. Banks?"

She looked at the nuns and smiled. They looked at each other and then smiled back at her. One of them went over to Rhoda Banks's bureau, opened a drawer, and took out a picture album. Rhoda Banks said to Chick, "My husband had a Brownie box camera. He knew how to develop film, too. He taught me."

And there, first with one brother and then with two, were pages and pages of the pretty little blond girl so many people held in their hearts, except that her hair was fine and straight. The last picture in the album was of Louise, her bright hair fit with a big bow, pulling her little brother in the new red Radio Flyer wagon he'd gotten for his birthday. Timmy had on a party hat. Bob stood off, the big brother, arms folded across his chest, surveying the scene. There was no question that Louise Banks was Little Miss 1565.

Bob said, "I want her to be with Timmy."

Chick said, "I'll start on that right now," and his voice was quaking so hard that Charlie went with him down the corridor to the phone. Margie was near the doorway so she heard Charlie say, "I'm gonna get the son of a bitch, Chick. I'm gonna get him."

Chapter Eleven

Margie had never been worried about Charlie before. Oh, she worried about him all the time because he was a fireman—he'd been burned several times. And he had a bad cough. Some fires he put out released blankets of asbestos dust onto him. But she'd never worried about his hobby. His hobby was not dangerous, his work was. The hobby was a game. Like Clue, Martha's favorite. But it should have ended. Life was divided into segments, after all. When you have a child, you see the segments clearly. Children finish with one and move into the next. Adults do the same thing. But Charlie's life was just one big section that didn't seem to have a finish. In fact, if anything, it had become more intense; Charlie himself had become more intense because of the Little Miss, who now had a name, and because of the arsonist, who now had a name as well—Louise's murderer. Charlie was more bent than ever on finding his firebug, whom he no longer called the Arsonist. Now it was Louise's Killer.

Margie decided to have a visit with her mother-in-law, Palma. Palma had lived alone since her husband died, the year Martha was born. But she didn't live alone the way Margie's father lived alone. She loved visitors; whoever came was welcome. That's because Denny O'Neill, when he was alive, had never let her have any friends. Not even visitors, except for her children when they'd grown up and no longer lived at home. He wasn't just an alcoholic, he was scum.

Margie asked Palma the kinds of things she'd asked her Aunt Jane about herself, only about Charlie. She asked, "Was Charlie always such a serious person?"

Palma said, "No."

Margie waited for more, but Palma had become busy breaking out the cannoli and getting the espresso machine cooking. When she'd put all the goodies in front of her daughter-in-law, she sat down across the table, and Margie asked, "When did he change?"

Palma cradled her cup in both hands as if she'd just come in from the cold. She said, "Margie, this new generation—Martha's and my other grandchildren's—they believe it is important to speak of any such thing that is troubling them. To talk those things out. My generation was taught that to let people see inside you was a sign of weakness."

Margie said, "And mine was in the middle. We never knew what to do so we just said anything or did anything without really thinking about it. The impulse generation."

"Yes. And now you've decided that Martha's has the right idea."

"I think so."

"You were always one to ask questions, though."

"I know. But that was just to hear myself think. I don't think I got good answers." And Margie thought of Baby

Pete, and the sperm, and the one-word answer that was all he needed.

Palma talked to Margie because she knew how much her daughter-in-law loved her son. When other people visited her, she'd flit around doing all sorts of things at once, but now she sat down and drank her coffee. She would talk to Margie.

"I don't like what's happening," Margie said.

"What's happening?"

"I'm beginning to look at Charlie in a new light."

Palma tossed a little grappa in their coffee, which was what her father used to do when he talked with his Abruzzi cronies. Before her husband died, when she'd make time for Margie, her eyes would keep shifting back and forth to be sure her husband wasn't hovering somewhere. When her little antennae told her he wanted something, she'd excuse herself and go to the bedroom or den and say, "Did you want something, Denny?" He always did. And when he didn't, he'd make up something. If she didn't stay a step ahead of him, he'd get especially ugly. He expected her to know what he wanted and when he wanted it, and she was able to do it, her intuition based on his location in the house, the tone of the grunts he emitted, and her cultural traditions.

Her eyes still shifted back and forth now and again—the habit so ingrained—but then she'd relax. She was no longer on call twenty-four hours a day. Also, now that the grappa was on a shelf next to the Crisco instead of hidden under the sink behind the hundred of bottles of cleaning fluids and powders, she'd take a hit quite often, not just with coffee. It loosened her up.

Margie said, "Palma, I didn't think an answer to my questions would mean that you'd have to expose something you don't want to expose."

Palma sighed. She ate another cannoli. She was so fat. She sighed again. She said, "Charlie was a happy baby. All my children were happy so long as they were small enough to fit into my arms. Then, after that, I couldn't protect them from their father. I thank God for my brothers who did." She made the sign of the cross over the expanse of her upper body.

Her brothers. Charlie and his own brothers adored them all, these Italian uncles who were all over six feet tall and who took after their mother from the Piedmont, strapping mountain climbers. One or another of them had been always at the ready, protecting their round little sister from the wrath of her husband. Charlie couldn't help but adore them, considering that his father was such a mean bastard. And then he came to truly love them because he realized that they'd have killed his father if the man laid a finger on their sister, saving Charlie and his brothers the trauma of having to do it themselves. The uncles respected their sister's marriage and never said a disapproving word to her, but they'd have thrown their brother-in-law in the Hog River if he'd touched her.

"Because of my brothers, Denny never hit the kids, but he was very cruel to them." Then she played with her fork, which was still clean. She'd shoveled the cannoli down her throat with her fingers. Her eyes were wet, though Palma, like Margie, wasn't a weeper.

Margie never wanted to hear about cruelty, but now she had no choice. Not if she really loved Charlie. She said, "What is it, Palma?"

Palma said, "People used to say he was mean because he was a drunk, but that wasn't so. His drinking gave him the excuse he needed to be mean. A built-in excuse: I had too much to drink so I can't help it if I'm mean. But, Margie, he *liked* being mean. The meaner he was, the more he enjoyed himself."

Margie could only think to say, "I'm so sorry, Palma."

Margie had once asked her, a long time ago, how she could

have stayed married to such a horrible man. That was before she found out about the tyranny of domestic economics from Martha. Palma had said that she stayed because the priests told women that men became mean when their wives riled them. How could you leave a man for being angry with you when you were the one who had brought on the anger? Treat your husband with kindness, they'd said, and he will, in turn, love and protect you. So she had maintained such a preposterous bargain only to realize that kindness is seen as stupidity by mean people and makes them even meaner.

The priests didn't know that when you're kind to a bully, the bully figures you're weak and worthless. That was because priests entered seminaries when they were fourteen years old. Once Margie said to Charlie that she hoped someday an archaeologist would find another 2,000-year-old scroll that said that Joseph beat the shit out of Mary when she told him she was pregnant. You want to get your boyfriend angry, tell him you're knocked up and that he's not the father. And at the time, Charlie got this look of wonder on his face, a look that didn't reflect Margie's, for a change. He said, "You know, it's true. People make believe you've gotten them angry so that they can get angry at you." Margie didn't know what he was talking about. She told Martha what he'd said. They had discussed the possible meanings. Then Martha had said, "Daddy really would like to open his mind. He would. But he can't because his *disk space* is full. Full of that circus shit. He's obviously capable of thinking provocatively. Something has actually managed to sneak into his brain that didn't have anything to do with that damn fire." But Margie could see that it would be hard for anything else to enter his mind, seeing as how he was married to a woman whose back was covered with the damn fire's scars. She didn't know about disk space.

The other reason Palma stayed with her husband was to avoid dishonor, the Italian code word.

"Margie?"

"Yes, Palma?"

"You've got that look."

"I know."

Palma meant that Margie looked bitter. No one else noticed, just Palma. Maybe Martha, too. Palma's generation got so much practice in reading other people's minds. The Palma generation figured that you were lazy and indifferent if you didn't make the time and effort to figure out what was bothering someone else. And then when you figured it out, you didn't bring up the topic; you just offered the person a cannoli.

Palma said to Margie, "All my children had to learn to tip-toe around their father. That will make a child serious."

"Palma, why did you marry your husband?"

Palma looked down into her cup. "Because he had a trade. He was a painter. He got steady work."

"But . . ."

"It was the Depression, Margie." Now she looked back up. "Have you come to tell me you're divorcing Charlie?"

"Palma!" Margie couldn't believe she'd said that. "Of course not. Charlie and I love each other."

"Then what is wrong, Margie?"

Margie started to say nothing, but that wouldn't have been fair. Palma had answered her; she should answer Palma. Margie refused to make Palma try to read her mind. Palma was a tired woman. She deserved peace. Margie said, "To tell the truth, Palma, I am really beginning to get damn sick and tired of this circus shit." Next, Margie was about to ask Palma her advice, but Palma suddenly reached across the table and gripped Margie's wrist. She said, "Get him to stop."

Get him to stop. To stop? Finding the pyromaniac was what Charlie was. Get him to stop, was sort of like, "Get him to shed his skin." Get the Statue of Liberty to put down the torch and give her arm a rest. And what about this divorce business? Had Palma read that from her vantage point across the table? Did Margie not know what was in her own mind? She was exasperated. So she called Martha at school. Charlie and Margie and their families referred to Yale as "school" so that they'd stop being awestruck. Martha was the one who had made the suggestion when she got tired of everyone being tongue-tied whenever they tried to get out the word *Yale*.

Martha happened to be in her room. "Are you in the mood to be my shrink for a few minutes, honey?"

Margie knew Martha had smiled. Martha said, "You're beginning to like searching your soul, right?"

"No."

"Oh, Mommy. I'm sorry. What's the matter?"

"I need to search my soul."

"You're a brave lady, Mom."

"I wish."

Margie told her about coffee with her grandmother.

"You want me to analyze Grandma's behavior?"

"Whatever."

"Well, hell. I don't know why she would say that. Nobody's going to get Daddy to stop, that's for sure. She must feel she knows something about you that isn't really there, or else something is there but you're not aware of it."

"But what should I do?"

"About what?"

"About figuring out what she was really saying."

"Mom. First of all, are you really sure she was trying to say something other than what she was saying?"

"Yes."

"You're getting good."

"Thanks."

"You could ask her, obviously."

"You know I can't."

"Yeah, right. Listen, Mom, you were a child when you met Grandma. Seventeen. That was me a year ago, right?"

"Yes." Incredible.

"So there's a good chance she knows things about you that you don't. Good chance."

"Martha?"

"What?"

"How's school?"

Long pause. "Great. I wish I didn't love calculus so much."

"So maybe you're not meant to be a lawyer."

"I'm meant."

"Is this calculus teacher a handsome man?"

Silence.

"Sorry, Martha. Didn't mean to read your mind."

Silence.

"I said I was sorry. But crushes are normal. And besides, when you develop a crush, you don't think: Gee, I guess I'll marry this guy and live happily ever after. Instead you think: He sure is cute. Period. Women of my generation envy that. We always thought in terms of, Is this the one? Really, Martha. No offense."

Martha laughed. "No offense taken. We're through with that other part of the conversation though, right? The part you called me about?"

"For now."

"Just think things through. Control those impulses."

"I will, baby."

Martha said, "Mom?"

"What, honey?"

"God! He is *so frigging cute!*"

Martha always knew when to let her mother off the hook, even though she did remind Margie on occasion that she had taken up with a man who was engaged to another woman. To everyone else in Margie's life, breaking another woman's engagement by stealing her man was shocking. No one ever brought it up. Not even while it was happening. Martha, however, found it very curious. Margie felt badly that Martha didn't see anything else about her that was intriguing, but that one bit of personal history did keep Martha from taking her for granted.

Margie took Martha's advice. She thought things through. She analyzed her relationship with her mother-in-law. She went back to the beginning. Those Sunday dinners were the beginning.

Margie had come to enjoy her new big family except for Charlie's father, whom she treated like a piece of furniture. She walked around him in her own brand of deference. He would look at Margie and she would look into the two holes that were his eyes. Every Sunday, he'd lurk, but then one Sunday he wasn't there. He'd never come home the night before. That had happened before, Margie was told, but by morning one or another of his buddies would arrive at the doorstep holding him up, and Palma and her sons would get him to the bathroom, where his wife would clean him. Charlie said to Margie that those times weren't so bad; it was when he'd come home still roaring drunk, stand in the living room, unzip his fly, and pee on the carpet. Now that was tough to take. Margie asked Charlie to please not tell her things like that, she couldn't stand it.

On this one Sunday everyone was getting ready for dinner and debating whether somebody should go look for him when the doorbell rang. Chick opened the door. Two of his friends, two cops, stood in the doorway. The crowd of people in the house flowed to the front door. Chick was whispering to the cops, and then he waved them off and turned.

"Denny's at the hospital."

Palma said, "Sweet mother of God."

Chick said, "He's dead."

Denny O'Neill had had a fight with his buddies and insisted on walking home from the bar just over the line in West Hartford. The dividing line between the two cities was the railroad tracks. He'd been hit by a freight train.

Margie watched the commotion that went on for days, and through all the telegrams and arrangements and visits from the priest, Margie especially watched Charlie. She couldn't take her eyes from his face, the face of a victor. The face of the warrior who's seen the enemy slain.

The final arrangements included the plan that Denny's sons should carry his coffin. Charlie said, "Not me."

The family enveloped Charlie. His mother begged him not to be bitter. His uncles spoke of scandal. His brothers told him to grow up. After all, this man was his father. Margie said to him, "I think you should do it for Palma."

So when Charlie said no to Margie, they all knew he meant it. There would be other pallbearers. The family was disgusted with Charlie, though. Margie said to him, "I respect you, Charlie, I do. If you can't do it, I know your reasons are right."

Charlie's eyes were clear. He said, "The filthy son of a bitch."

As it turned out, Charlie didn't even go to the funeral.

Now in thinking all that through, it wasn't Charlie's father whom Margie was imagining. The burned out holes instead of eyes had become her own father's. There was nothing there in Jack Potter's eyes anymore. Not when Margie stood watching him from the door of his room. But when he spotted her, they would fill with duty, and with affection, if not love. Love had been taken from him by the war, though Jack Potter blamed something else. The psychiatrist said to Margie, "If a prisoner of war is liberated, he leaves his prison with nothing. In a way, putting it simply, he's almost like a baby being born. He has to find out who he is. Most are able to do it, though it is a great burden to them since it forces them to relive what they wish they could forget. But, of course, they can't forget even if they want to. Your mother was an excuse for your father not to have to relive what he'd been through."

Margie said, "I think it's too late to do anything about that."

The doctor said, "I'm afraid that's true. I wish it wasn't so."

"Me too."

Margie wondered at what point it had been too late for her father-in-law to get out of the hellhole he was in. Margie had never had a single conversation with Denny O'Neill; she'd just said that one word to him. Lush. Her own father didn't initiate conversations with his daughter, but he answered everything she asked, and paid attention, in a hazy way, to things she told him. When Margie was twelve, she read *The Diary of a Young Girl*. Margie didn't know how it would end. As she read it, she couldn't wait to get to that final scene when the Americans would invade Europe and save the day: She could just see the GIs crashing into the Annex to rescue the Franks, the van Damms, and Mr. Dussel; then Anne and Peter going out on a real date; Anne's sister, Margot, finding a boyfriend of her own. But when Margie finished the book, she couldn't believe the ending that she'd found there—no ending—and was horrified as she read the afterword. She ran downstairs and said to her father, "Did you know that Hitler tried to kill every Jew in the world, even the kids?" She waved the book at him. "Even Anne Frank?"

He said yes, of all things, and that was more of a shock than the horrendous secret Margie had come upon. Her father was in on it.

"You knew about it?"

"Yes."

"How come you didn't tell me?"

He said, "Same reason your schoolbooks won't tell you. People think it's best to isolate children from the truth. That's why teenagers go wild. They find out the truth and are rightfully angry that it was kept from them. People are very stupid, Margie. Especially the smart ones."

She'd gone back to her room to think. Twelve-year-olds do a lot of thinking because no one ever tells them anything, as her father had just pointed out. She began to see that this Jew-killing was kept from kids for the same reason sex was hidden. People didn't tell their children about the Nazis killing the Jews because maybe kids would think that if adults did things as bad as that, why wouldn't they?

Margie had learned about sex two years before. Her father had given her a book on menstruation. Margie tended to skim-read when she was reading something exciting. She could read an Agatha Christie in forty-five minutes. Her brain automatically condensed books the way Reader's Digest does for people who don't have the natural ability. So she skimmed the menstruation book, learning first of all that Modess rhymed with, *Oh yes,* no exclamation point. When she finished it, she held the mind-boggling notion that girls bled from all their pores once a month and wrapped these bandages that rhymed with *Oh yes* around their arms and legs and bodies, and presumably, during that time of the month, went around in long-sleeved shirts and dungarees. (Not only did Margie skim, she filled in pertinent information that she inevitably missed.) But what about your face and hands? she wondered. She wondered about logistics rather than the female body's need to rid itself of a gallon of blood every twenty-eight days. (The book had said *pint,* but she'd skimmed by that.)

Margie, being a Catholic, accepted the whole thing as some kind of stigmata, which the nuns told the children in catechism class was an especially wonderful gift of God bestowed on the very, very few. Margie's nun, at the time, had looked down at her own unblessed palms soulfully.

Margie ran across the street to her friend Julie's house and shoved the pamphlet under her nose. But Julie knew all about it already, and proceeded to set Margie straight on where the blood actually came out. The place she told Margie the blood came out seemed far more outrageous than Margie's pores idea. Margie told her friend that she had to use the bathroom, and she went in, pulled down her pants, put Julie's mother's magnified makeup mirror on the floor, and squatted over it. Then she ran back out and said, "Julie! Why didn't you tell me?"

Julie said, "My mother told me she'd kill me if I told any of my friends because it's up to their mothers to tell them."

Margie said, "I don't have a mother."

"Oh, yeah. I forgot."

Julie didn't have a father. He had died of a heart attack when she was five. But she could remember him, at least. Now Margie looked back at the kids on her street where she grew up. Every one of them came from what would now be labeled a dysfunctional family, but no one knew the word *functional*, let alone *dysfunctional*, so no one felt deprived. There was Margie whose mother was dead, and Julie whose father was dead. And Margie would never forget the thrilling day she was down the street at her friend Barbara's house and the police came to the kitchen door.

They banged on the door so hard Margie couldn't imagine why they didn't break through—something so easily accomplished by Mickey Spillane. She and Barbara were at the kitchen table writing to their pen pals in Egypt, and Barbara's dad sat across from them and it looked to Margie like he was writing to a pen pal, too. Barbara's mother was at the stove slicing carrots into a pot. After those initial shouts of, "Open up! Police!" there was an instant when Barbara's kitchen became a tableau. Margie could picture exactly when she and Barbara and Barbara's parents all looked into each other's eyes at the same time. Then Barbara's mother ran to the door and pretended she couldn't open it while Barbara's father started ripping up the pieces of paper he'd been writing on. Then he started eating the pieces. Barbara grabbed more of his papers, handed Margie a bunch, and said, "C'mon, Margie. C'mon, c'mon." Margie ran with her, following her to the bathroom, tearing up papers the whole while. Margie did the same to the letter to her pen pal, which she had in her hand. In the bathroom, Barbara flushed away all the little pieces of paper. Then she grabbed Margie's arm and dragged her back to the kitchen table and said, "Write."

Margie could hear Barbara's father charging down the cellar stairs. Then Barbara's mother wiped off her hands on her apron, smiled, and said cheerfully, "Well, here we go," and she opened the door. Two policemen fell through, looked around, ran in and out of every room in the house, down and back up the cellar stairs, and then they ran back out. Barbara's mother shut the door behind them and said to Barbara and Margie, "Now that the stew's out of the way, would you girls like to make a nice refrigerator cake?"

When Margie got home, carrying a piece of cake Barbara's mother insisted she bring to her father, she told him what happened. He put down his magazine and said, "Well, I guess I won't hit the double today. Not that I ever have it, anyway." Then he described to Margie the profession of booking horses. Definitely dysfunctional, Margie now knew.

Her friend Pidgie, whose house was a little farther down the street from Barbara's, lived with her aunt and uncle, who were from Sweden. They didn't call her Pidgie, though. The kids in the neighborhood made up that name because they couldn't pronounce her real name and because she tamed a pigeon that would land on her shoulder when she called him. Then there was Carol, who was adopted and whose parents were very old. And next to Carol, Barry, who had a sister who was a mongoloid who also had a hole in her heart and was addicted to Cokes. She sucked at the Cokes through a big nipple that her mother would pull onto the bottles for her. And Artie's parents were divorced at a time when only movie stars were divorced, and Johnny's grandmother had a nervous breakdown so she had to sleep in his room on a cot while she got better. Then there was Poor Barry. Never just "Barry." He wasn't allowed out to play. He could only study and practice his violin. Once Margie and her friends went en masse to his house and told his mother they were desperate for one more ballplayer. She gave in to their pleas and her son's tears but she told Poor Barry that he couldn't use the children's bats. He'd have to use the one she'd gotten him. It was a souvenir bat from the Statue of Liberty, twelve inches long.

All of the kids in the neighborhood were not terribly concerned about any of this. They'd tease each other once in a while, and say things like: "Hey, Johnny, does your grandmother snore?" Or, "Pidgie, you ever get sick of Swedish meatballs?" But nobody seemed to ask why Johnny's grandmother had a nervous breakdown or where Pidgie's parents were. Like Jack Potter said, children were isolated from the truth. They were not encouraged to think. In fact, after explaining why the cops broke down Barbara's door, Jack Potter said, "Best to forget about the whole thing. Just keep on being Barbara's friend." So Margie never said anything to Barbara about the incident, and Barbara never said anything to Margie.

But then when kids start to get a little older, they get surprises more far-reaching than a friend's father being a bookie. Like Anne Frank. She was from a dysfunctional country. She was my childhood trauma, Margie told herself, not my mother being dead, not my father being a hermit. So Margie had promised herself that when she had children, they would know the truth. Now she had one and she did know everything. Margie had told Martha about sex from the time she was little. Martha at ten had been nothing like Margie at ten. Give her an answer, you'd get another question. At ten, she'd said, "So how does a baby fit through this hole?"

Margie told her the hole stretched. Martha said, "Oh, yeah. Right."

When Vietnam came along, Martha and her fellows were up to the challenge.

Once Margie was watching a sports talk show. Dick Schaap and Joe Namath were talking about the Franco Zeffirelli film *Romeo and Juliet*. Joe found the plot very upsetting and said he didn't like such depressing movies. Dick Schaap kind of looked out at the audience and then back at Joe. Then he said, "You didn't know how it would end, did you, Joe?" And Joe said, "How could I know how it'd end? I just seen it." That was about the only time ever that Margie figured it was advantageous to not know what life was all about. Lucky Joe. Shakespeare as thriller seemed a good idea to her. Margie wished she didn't know what happened to Anne Frank.

Chapter Twelve

During the time Martha was away at school, Margie got another one of those Anne Frank kind of surprises. From Charlie. Charlie told her that Chick's wife, Aunt Annette, had finally brought herself to the point where she was able to talk about the fire.

Margie asked, "What does she want to talk about?"

"About what it was like for her. Aunt Annette was there."

Margie repeated the words, though they came out a question. "Aunt Annette was there?"

Charlie said, "Yes. She's finally able to discuss her experience. After all these years."

Now Margie said words of her own, but they were framed in another question. "Aunt Annette was at the circus?"

"Yes. And Cindy and Ruth-Ann."

"Cindy and Ruth-Ann?" She was back to repeating.

Charlie said, "Jesus, what's the matter with you?"

Margie actually began to say: What's the matter with *me*? But she didn't. She just stared at him. His face was concerned, as always, but his eyes were innocent. Innocent, goddamn it. She said, "Charlie, it's the same as lying."

"What's the same as lying?"

"Not being frank. Deliberately not being frank. It's worse than lying."

He went into a spiel. A planned-out spiel, Margie could tell. Prepared, like Martha's briefs. He had known she would be hurt when he told her about Annette. Hurt, but according to Charlie's definition. Hurt feelings, like when a child learns a secret has been kept from her. Betrayed, according to Margie—like Anne Frank. So he began to talk to her as if she were a child, filling her in on the details she knew nothing about. All the while, Margie kept thinking, What is happening here? Why did he hide this from me? She tried to listen to him.

"See, Margie, Uncle Chick was in a patrol car on the day of the fire. The dispatcher called every cop on patrol to tell them something was going on at the circus and to get over there. So while he was heading toward Barbour Street, the dispatcher said, 'The tent's on fire.' Chick got there five minutes later. The fire had began ten minutes before that so by the time he got there, the tent was gone."

He looked at Margie and waited for her to ask a question. She didn't. He answered the question he'd expected her to ask. "It didn't take him very long to find them, thank God."

He waited. He said, "Uncle Chick didn't find Little Miss 1565's mother, though. Not for a long time."

Margie's despair at Charlie was mixed with thoughts of Chick walking amidst the fire equipment, ambulances, and the cars driving up, and all the jeeps sent over from Brainard Field full of soldiers coming to help out. She knew that he probably spent a lot of time, himself, helping out, not knowing if Annette and his little girls were under the smoking ashes, as Louise Banks was. Then he found them. So that explained Uncle Chick. But that didn't explain Charlie. Margie's instinct was to jump up and call Martha and say, "Aunt Annette and Cindy and Ruth-Ann were at the circus!" But she didn't. Because Martha wouldn't comment on what those words were all about, or why her father never mentioned to her mother that piece of the fire puzzle. Instead, Martha would address the wound of betrayal in her mother's voice. And Margie couldn't face that.

"Margie, honey," Charlie asked, "is anything wrong?"

"No."

Aunt Annette and Cindy and Ruth-Ann arrived with a pan of lasagna from Palma. Aunt Annette said, "A little something to heat up after, Margie."

Margie thanked her. "Stay and have some with us when we finish."

Ruth-Ann said, "Yeah, let's, Ma. Daddy'll be okay. He'll make a salami sandwich." To Margie, she said, "When your father's a policeman it seems normal when he's not at dinner." Then to her mother, "He'll have his sandwich and a beer and listen to the Sox."

Cindy didn't say a thing. She never did. She was an introvert, the only introvert in Charlie's family.

Aunt Annette agreed. Margie put the lasagna in the oven and went up to the war room after the rest of them. Before she could even click on the tape recorder, Aunt Annette was saying, "The Chief got fifty free tickets. He gave four to Chick. But he was on duty that day. You—"

Charlie said, "I need you to show me a few things first, Aunt Annette." He'd interrupted her. He'd never interrupted his witnesses. Margie guessed he felt he could since this was his aunt.

But then Ruth-Ann interrupted. She was looking around, "You've expanded since last time I was here, huh, Charlie?"

"Yeah."

She rolled her eyes. Ruth-Ann was not sensitive to humoring Charlie—she just did it. Family loyalty.

Right away, Annette started to say again, "Chick was on duty that day, so he couldn't come with us. That's why you . . ."

She took a Kleenex and looked down on it. Then she looked up at Charlie. She started wringing the Kleenex in her hands. She wanted him to interrupt her.

Charlie said, "Go ahead, Aunt Annette. It's okay."

She said, "Our extra ticket. We gave it to a little boy on Barbour Street. You . . ."

"It really is all right. You can tell me."

"Charlie, I'm sure that boy didn't . . ."

Margie said, "What little boy?"

Ruth-Ann said, "You want me do this, Charlie? Maybe I'll remember something else."

Charlie said, "I remember everything you told me on that day. Everything." Charlie turned to Margie. "The girls and Aunt Annette came to stay with us that night. Ma didn't want them to be alone since Chick couldn't come home. Ruth-Ann talked half the night. Cindy was only four."

Cindy's eyes darted about. She didn't like this.

Annette said, "Charlie, I came here to say something. I have to tell you the truth. I came, not because I thought I could help you find out who set the fire. I came to try to help you in . . . in other ways."

Now she brought the Kleenex up to her eyes. Ruth-Ann snatched another Kleenex from the pop-up box and gave it to her mother so she'd have a Kleenex for her other hand. Charlie started to speak. Annette waved her new Kleenex at him.

"No, no. I have something to say. Something to explain to

you. I was so angry, Charlie. I was so angry by the time we got to the circus, I couldn't see straight. I wanted to kill your father. And I was even angrier at your mother for not standing up to him. But that boy we gave your ticket to . . . Charlie, after all these years, I went and looked at the names of the boys who died. I was always so afraid to know if he'd died. But I had to know before I could come to you.

"None of the dead were from the neighborhood. And that boy definitely was. I saw him come out of his house on Barbour Street. He didn't die. And . . . I felt so much better to know . . . he'd been so happy to get the ticket. So happy. The way you'd been, too. He kept saying, 'Oh, thank you, lady, thank you, lady.' He was not killed by the fire, thank God."

The day Margie met Charlie, he told her he'd had a ticket to the circus but didn't go. Now she was finding out that he hadn't been joking after all. He really had had a ticket. But he'd told Margie the truth back then in such a tone that he knew she would think he was joking.

Margie said, "Let me get this right. Charlie, you had a ticket to the circus, but your father took it away."

"I thought you knew that, Margie."

Margie wondered why he would lie. She said to her aunt, "Do you think Charlie is trying to find the arsonist because he feels guilty about the boy you gave the ticket to? That the boy might have died?"

"Yes, oh, yes. That's what I came here to say. I finally found the courage to see if a boy from Barbour Street died. But he didn't."

Aunt Annette's theory wasn't right, Margie was sure of that. Margie tried to catch Charlie's eye but couldn't. Charlie said, "Aunt Annette, I've checked, too. I checked a long time ago. I know the boy didn't die in the fire."

"You checked?"

"Of course."

"Then why are you doing this?"

Ruth-Ann said, "I told you, Ma. Because he's Charlie. Because our Daddy is really his Daddy. His own was a dud. He's a chip off the old block—our Daddy's block, not his Daddy's block. The brilliant Martha would tell us that, right Margie?"

Ruth-Ann was always jealous about Martha because her own children were such a disappointment to her. Cindy touched her mother's arm. She said softly, "Tell Charlie what you saw at the circus. If you want to help him, then just tell him what he's asking you to tell him."

Annette refocused on the Kleenex. "I didn't come to encourage him."

Charlie said, "Aunt Annette. I know you worry about me. I'm all right, though. Some people believe the fire was an accident. I don't. I just want to prove I'm right."

She sighed. "Okay then. You always want to know where people were sitting, isn't that right?"

"Yes."

"But you know where we were sitting."

"Yes."

Margie looked at the Map. She interrupted. "I don't know where. Charlie, why aren't their names on the wall?"

He said, "I know their seats. One of them was supposed to be mine."

Annette said, "We were way over at the end of the tent— the opposite end from where the fire started. Near the bandstand. The music was very loud where we were, but I didn't care. All I knew was that I wanted . . . I wanted to strangle your father, Charlie, for not letting you come with us. I can still see your little face. . . ."

"What did you see from your seat near the bandstand?"

She breathed heavily. "First, I heard people yelling: 'Fire, fire!' And then everyone began to stand and point. I saw the little circle of flame. It seemed little because the tent was so big. But when I saw it, the circle must have been three or four feet across. The band stopped what they were playing and went into the 'Stars and Stripes.'"

"Just before you heard someone yell fire, what did you see?"

"I watched the lady getting the lions and tigers out of the cage and down the chute. She was a little bit of a thing, but the lions and tigers jumped off their stools one at a time and ran right through the chute. And the big spotlight went on, aimed at the top of the tent. The center peak of the tent. The Wallendas had already climbed up their ladder. The sun was so bright that day that the Wallendas didn't have shadows. The way they do at night. At a night performance, the big spotlight makes huge shadows of the performers against the tent. I used to love the circus, Charlie."

Margie said, "My mother loved the circus. My father told me."

And now, along with his aunt's and cousins', Charlie's eyes shifted to Margie's. Cindy said, "We love you, Margie."

Cindy had said those same words to her the day Charlie told his family he had broken his engagement to Sylvia and was marrying someone else, and then introduced the some-one else. Cindy, who never talked, made sure she let Margie know that everything was all right. Now Cindy's eyes and Charlie's bore into one another's. Ruth-Ann said, "Jesus, Cindy, you're still some kind of hippie."

Cindy's eyes shifted back down to her feet. Annette ignored this. There was nothing she could do about having two children who were opposites. Charlie said, "Go ahead, Aunt Annette."

Little shreds of Kleenex were spread across her lap. "The Wallendas looked so tiny up there. Like little toy soldiers. One of them was a lady. The men were dismantling the ani-mal cage. The cage took up the whole ring. When the last tiger was into the chute, the men were already taking the cage apart."

Margie said, "Leopard."

Annette said, "Whatever. The men took the cage down as fast as the Wallendas climbed their ladder. The first thing I thought when I saw the fire was that at least the animals wouldn't be trapped in the cage. I never dreamed it would be the people who were trapped."

Charlie filled in the pause. "So people began to point."

"Yes. At the little circle of fire. For those few seconds everyone waited for someone to put it out. But no one had a chance to put it out. In the next second, the circle turned into one big long pillar of fire straight up the whole side of the tent. Like a streak of lightning, only straight, and then the band broke into the 'Stars and Stripes.' They played it real loud. I grabbed the girls' hands and ran around the grandstand. We were in the front row because we had the police tickets. When we got around the grandstand, the whole top of the tent was one big sheet of fire, and at that point, the pieces of canvas—burning pieces—began to come down. To this day, I don't know how the Wallendas got out. But they did. I didn't see anything. Someone had cut the tent behind the grandstand with a jackknife. We slipped through the cut. Then I ran with the girls."

"You were one of the first to get out."

"Yes."

"And what did you see?"

"People running. Just like us. We ran to the edge of the lot and then I had to sit down. I held the girls' heads in my lap and I watched the circus burn to the ground. It looked like the newsreels. Like a whole street in London, firebombed. Except it was daytime and it was a circus tent. And the band kept playing and playing. The music made it seem like the whole thing was a terrible nightmare; as long as the band played it couldn't be real. That's what I kept thinking: This is just the newsreel; in a minute, the movie will come on. Isn't that so foolish?"

Charlie said, "A lot of people told me they thought of it as a newsreel. Aunt Annette, did you see any people near the tent who were not acting the way everyone else was acting?"

Now she looked up. "No, Charlie. I never saw what you're wanting someone to see. I couldn't take my eyes off the tent, though. I couldn't look away. Everyone else was looking away, but not me. Maybe because I hadn't been enjoying the circus. Your father saw to it that you missed out on everything. Everything! And your mother, God forgive me, she—"

"What happened next?"

"Next? The tent began to sway. The two ends of the tent disintegrated, but the center pole swayed for what seemed like such a long time and then it came down. Just before it fell is when the music finally stopped. The musicians all ran out of the tent and ran to a place right near where we were sitting. They set up their instruments and they started playing again. They had their drums and cymbal stands with them and everything. The backs of their red uniforms were all black. I said to the girls, 'See, everyone got out okay.'"

Cindy's little voice arose. "But that wasn't so."

"No, it wasn't. Then the pole fell and what was left of the tent fell with it. Everything was flat and black and smoldering and the only thing left standing was the Wallendas' platform. It was way high up against the sky and I knew then how dangerous their act was. All alone, against the sky, the platform seemed a mile high. But then it toppled, and when it did all the screaming and the music, too, was drowned out by the sounds of sirens. So I told the girls that their Daddy was coming to find us, that he would have to do his duty first, though. He did. He did his duty and then he found us." She looked up. Her face was covered with tears. "That's everything I remember."

And then Margie waited for Charlie to ask his aunt what

she remembered before the fire. When she and the girls had arrived. They'd skipped that part. But he didn't ask. So Margie did. She said, "Aunt Annette, before the fire, was anyone walking around the tent? Someone acting strangely? Carrying something that seemed not to belong?"

Cindy excused herself and left the room. She'd been four years old. What horrible things did she hold inside? Annette lifted her head. "No, honey. Just everyone all excited about going to the circus." She turned to Charlie once more. "You'll never find him. Six thousand people were there. Another couple hundred performers and hands. You won't do it, and what if you do? The dead will stay dead and Little Miss 1565 won't come back to her mother." She turned to Margie. "And your poor dear mother won't come back to you. It's a long time now. A long time."

Charlie said, "You're married to a cop, Aunt Annette. What's the time limit on justice?"

She said, "Don't you dare lecture me, Charlie. I do believe in justice. I do. But I also believe that if there was an arsonist, he was caught when he went and set another fire. Besides, arsonists are sick people. They can't really help what they're doing. Finding a mentally ill person is not justice. Justice is seeing that circus tents don't get waterproofed with gasoline ever again."

Charlie didn't address that. Never had. That was not justice. He said, "People know right from wrong. Especially after they've killed a hundred and sixty-nine people, and scarred a couple thousand more."

From Charlie's face, Margie could see that he wanted to argue some more, but he had too much respect for his family. And Annette hadn't said anything important to him, anyway. As far as what she'd seen at the circus, there was certainly nothing new. Of course, there wouldn't be. It was just the same thing over and over again. Palma was right. It was time to get him to stop. Margie realized that, and Annette could see it. Maybe Palma had spoken to her, too. Margie thought: And I'm no goddamn different from Palma. Margie felt as if she were just like the wife of any alcoholic, putting up with abnormal behavior out of some sort of screwed-up version of love that looked like, and felt like, and smelled like loyalty, but was something else. Margie had no idea what.

Margie was not a manipulator. She got no pleasure from power struggles. She would not connive to get Charlie to stop; she would not pussyfoot around. She had no interest in saying one thing that really meant another thing. Margie was able to admit to herself, though, that thoughts of making Charlie's favorite dessert and buying a special bottle of wine did enter her mind, but she kicked it all out and left her mind clear.

So when she and Charlie went to bed that night, she said, "Charlie, I don't want you to do this anymore. I don't want to hear the words *circus* and *fire* next to each other again. I want all this to be over. I want to turn your room into a guest room for Martha—something pretty for when she comes back on her breaks."

"Martha has a room."

"She'll need a bigger one when she's got a husband. And her room can be for the babies."

Charlie, the great compromiser, mentioned to his wife that she was getting ahead of herself. Margie said, "But I can't wait anymore."

"For me to find him?"

"No, Charlie. For you to stop trying."

So he said, "Give me a year, Margie."

Margie said, "Sure." She'd hoped there'd be a compromise, as there had always been, and she leaped at this one. What's a year compared with all that's gone before? Then she said, "Tell me what it is you're after. Tell me. And if you say justice, I'll spit in your eye."

"You don't believe I'm after justice? Since when?"

"Since Louise Banks was identified. That's enough justice to go around. That's all anyone needs to close the book."

"There's one more chapter to this book."

"And if the arsonist's dead? If you find him and he's dead, what are you going to do? Dig him up and have him arrested? Electrocuted?"

Margie felt Charlie turn toward her in the dark. She waited, but he didn't say anything. She said, "Charlie, I'm sorry. I didn't mean to be sarcastic. I was trying to make a point."

Charlie tried to make a point. "Why don't you want to find out who did this to you?"

"Did *what* to me? There's nothing *wrong* with me. You've got me all wrapped up in this because you think there's something wrong with me. But I was a *baby*, Charlie. I don't remember the pain I felt. I don't remember anything. I'm happy! I've got all that I ever wanted."

"Is what it did to your father all you ever wanted?"

A lump rose in Margie's throat. She would not let him catch her. "The war is what happened to my father."

"All right, then—somebody killed your mother and got away with it. Do you want that?"

"I don't remember her!"

"Even if you don't remember her, somebody killed her. And if she'd been there for your father when he got home, maybe his life wouldn't have been destroyed."

"But it's too late now. He's not going to change."

"But I'll change."

And that, she knew, was Charlie's justice. Some kind of personal vendetta. Maybe the damned Abruzzi roots just came out stronger in Charlie than the rest of the family. Margie said, "Charlie, another year. And I know that it won't be as simple as you're trying to make me believe it is. This stuff isn't some little hobby. When it's gone, you won't just be able to turn around and take up fishing instead. You hate to fish, remember?"

He said, "Yeah."

"You must promise me to get this all out of your head and find the reasons for why you've been obsessed with that circus. We'll go to a psychiatrist together, Charlie. Martha will tell us how to do that. You need some peace. And so do I. I really believe . . . I mean I really believe, Charlie, that even if you find the arsonist in the next year, you still won't have peace."

Charlie said, "I'll do anything for you, Margie. But I will have peace. I deserve to find out who set that fire. I deserve it!"

"I deserve peace, too."

"Yes, you do. I love you."

He loved her. And he loved lying next to her naked, tracing her scars with his fingertips. Or with his tongue.

Chapter Thirteen

This July 6, Uncle Chick and a few thousand others went to Little Miss 1565's new grave. Her real name was on the clean white marble headstone. There had been some discussion as to whether the headstone should also say Little Miss 1565, but her mother and brother were adamant. They wanted her to have a normal rest. Next to her stone was a little marker for her brother, Timmy—his name, his birthdate, and the date of his death, the same day as his sister's. Chick, together with Rhoda Banks, put white roses on the boy's grave and yellow roses on Louise's. Yellow, her mother told the reporters, had been Louise's favorite color. The headline in the Hartford *Courant* read NO MORE FORGET-ME-NOTS FOR LOUISE.

Charlie was not there. Every year, on the anniversary of the fire, Charlie worked a double shift. He'd told Margie a long time ago that on that particular day, he wanted to make sure any fires that started in Hartford got put out before anyone died.

Martha had come home for the ceremony. That was because the Little Miss seemed like part of her own family. Martha wanted to be there for her Great-uncle Chick when he buried his other little girl. She and Margie held hands during the prayers, and Margie wondered if Martha might just be grieving for brothers and sisters she'd never had. Then she also wondered if she herself wasn't grieving for other little girls she could have had. Little Pete's kids were lined up all in a row. When the crowd broke up, chatting and drifting off to their cars, Margie just stood, taking in the gently rolling hills of Saint Bartholemew's cemetery in Hartford's North End, just half a mile from where the circus had burned.

Martha said, "Mom, you ready to go?"

Margie said, "When I was little, Aunt Jane used to drive me here and we'd put flowers on my mother's grave."

"What?"

"We used to come here."

"My *grandmother* is buried here?"

"Yes."

"But you never told me that. You never brought me here."

"I know. That's because I didn't feel anything. I'd stand there with Jane and Little Pete wishing I were at the playground instead, on the seesaw or the swings. I couldn't wait to get back to the car and read my book."

Martha said, "Then it did mean something, Mom. Wishing you were flying through the air on a swing sounds like a great escape to me. 'Course we all know about reading."

"Reading?"

"As an escape. But, shoot, Mom, let's go see her."

Margie said, "I have no idea where she is."

"Then we'll find out."

They drove along the narrow gravel drive and came to the

caretaker's cottage. He gave them a map and pointed out BE891. Margie asked, "My mother's name isn't on the gravestone?"

He said, "Times were tough then."

She turned to Martha, "I guess I'd forgotten that there was no name."

Margie and Martha found her in a part of the cemetery with no tombstones, just long rows of rectangular bricks of granite. They walked the B row until they came to BE891. Martha said, "I think we should get her something better."

Margie started to say yeah, but nothing came out.

Martha said, "Mom, I don't know who this woman is."

"No one does, really. She came from the Midwest. Her family disowned her."

Martha looked into her mother's eyes. "Disowned her? What the hell is that supposed to mean?"

Margie said, "I don't know, honey. That's what Grandpa told me."

"Jesus, Mom. The Midwest? That's a fairly big area. What state? And who the hell disowns people these days?" Martha folded her arms across her chest. "I mean, besides the wackos in your Jackie Collins books."

"Martha, what is the matter with you? You're shouting at me."

Martha sagged. "Oh, Mom, I'm sorry."

"I don't know why I never asked about those things."

"Mom, how about we go visit Grandpa?"

Margie looked down at her mother's grave. "Yes. I think we should."

Margie followed her daughter, who stepped briskly, toward the one-year-old Coupe de Ville, which was ready to be traded in.

Jack Potter said, "We were students. She was very young. We had three weeks until I had to go overseas."

Margie didn't hear him after the word *students*. "Students?"

Martha said, "Students at college, Grandpa?"

Her grandfather said to her, "Of course, Martha."

Margie excused herself, said she'd be right back. She went out into the corridor and leaned on the wall. After a few moments, Martha came out for air, too. "Mom?"

"I don't know what he's talking about."

"Mom, he just told me he was at Columbia. And get ready for this—she was at Barnard."

"My God."

"I can't believe we never knew this. He never said anything?"

Margie didn't answer because she was thinking. Why didn't her father tell her she should go to college? Her mother had. Martha didn't notice her mother not responding to her.

"Jesus, he never even said anything when I went to Yale. C'mon, Mom, let's go back in and get the rest."

Margie followed her. "Here's Mom, Grandpa. I told her you went to Columbia. She can't believe you never told her that."

He said, "I'm sorry, Margie."

Margie thought of all those nights at dinner. Reading. Columbia, to Margie, sounded a lot like *suttee*.

Martha was excited. "Tell us, now, Grandpa. I really want to know—I mean, I have a right to know who my grandmother was."

"She was very young." Jack Potter closed his eyes. "The second we found each other we breathed the same air."

Martha turned to gape at her mother.

"We got married by a justice of the peace. The first letter that reached me, she told me we were having a child. It was what we both hoped for."

Martha said, "That's when her family disowned her?"

"No. That happened when she told them she was marrying me."

"Why would they do that? Because you were going overseas?"

"Because they were Orthodox Jews."

Jack Potter's room became still. The stir of the window fan was the only sound, the only movement. Then Jack Potter picked up his newspaper and started to read. He squinted. His eyes were finally going. Last.

Outside, back in the car, Martha said, "Maybe he made all that up."

Margie said. "Then what would the real story be?"

"Do you mind if I find out?"

Margie started to cry. Martha held her in her arms. She said to her mother, "I wish I could think of what I should say. But I just can't imagine what it would be like to be a child whose mother died so tragically. Especially when the child knows that the mother died because she was trying to save her. That's why you don't know about her. You had to distance yourself. Now it's just all coming down on you at once, Mom. Take it easy."

Margie said, "If she'd had been in Europe instead of here, she'd have died practically the same way."

"Jesus, Mom."

"This is all so awful, Martha. I don't know what horrible things happened to Grandpa in the war. He was 'captured.' What the hell is 'captured' supposed to mean?"

"Listen, at least we know why he is the way he is. Whatever he saw he's still seeing."

"He looks very old, doesn't he?"

"Yes."

"Let's go."

When Martha visited Barnard to learn about her grandmother, and while Margie was arranging for a stone for her mother, Jack Potter died. His daughter didn't need him anymore. Margie and her Aunt Jane and her uncle, Big Pete, decided it would be best to move his wife so that the two of them could be together. There was no room in the row of granite blocks for another grave. The children of Martha Potter's brothers and sisters, most of them still living in the Jewish neighborhood in Omaha where their long-dead aunt grew up, offered their sympathies to Margie through her daughter.

Charlie, when he learned all this, whispered to Margie, "This is the year we're going to get him."

Martha escaped back to school.

Charlie had started up a new notebook listing what he planned to do each day during his last six months. "I'm consolidating," he told Margie, who was too numb to notice his excitement. This new determination brought on by Margie's hard-line ultimatum had inspired him. While his family mourned the loss of his father-in-law, he began taking on new energy. He intended to do in six months what he'd been trying to do since he joined the fire department as a very young man. And then a phone call came. Early even for a fireman's phone, and it brought Margie out of what everyone was calling her "doldrums." It was Chick telling Charlie that an inmate at the Brampton Penitentiary for the Criminally Insane had confessed to setting the fire. "Brampton," Chick said, "is in Canada."

The inmate's name was Henry Maxson. He was serving a murder conviction for the torture-slaying of two people. He'd forced a young couple at gunpoint into a gardening shed, locked it, and set it on fire. That was all Chick knew right then. Chick immediately went about fixing things up between the Hartford Police Department and the Canadian warden in order to get Charlie the information on the guy. Then Chick called back. All Margie heard of the phone conversation was Charlie saying either, "Yep," or "I know that." Then he hung up and told her what Chick had said, but she already knew that all the "Yep"s were Charlie taking in the facts, and all the "I know that"s had to do with Chick reminding him that the guy had made the confession three days after the anniversary of the fire when national newspapers and TV newscasts were full of the accounts of Little Miss 1565's final resting place.

"Louise," Margie said. Charlie said, "Yeah, Louise."

Chick called back a third time. Charlie listened for a moment and then passed the receiver to Margie. Chick dictated a plan, which Margie transcribed into the appropriate folder. Once again, Margie was smack in the middle of a Robert Ludlum/Ken Follett action thriller. She was indispensable. The adventure was back on. Margie felt released.

She coordinated the plan. Charlie would fly up to Canada accompanied by a Hartford fire marshal whose job was investigating arson, along with a detective from the police department who was an old friend of Chick's. This particular detective had gotten a big promotion the day before Chick retired. Chick had spent the last week before he retired making sure he'd paid back all the favors he owed, and adding a few new favors just for insurance. Chick had insurance policies in a lot of places. Now he'd put in a claim. Too much red tape to try to do it directly through the police department, Charlie told Margie.

Margie would go, too, compliments of the Cadillac Seville she wouldn't be getting, after all. She was a little disappointed. She'd heard that next year's Seville would look like an upside-down bathtub just like all the other cars on the road, and the one she'd be turning in for cash looked like a British roadster. She'd felt like Harriet Vane when she'd taken it out for a test drive, off to rendezvous with Lord Peter.

Chick fixed things up so well that the warden of the penitentiary agreed to meet with their contingent right away, and, depending on how Henry was feeling, Charlie might be able to interview him. "Depending on how Henry was feeling . . ." struck delicious terror into Margie's heart. How do people feel who set fire to other people? They would fly out at the end of the week, early Thursday morning, so on Wednesday, the fire marshal, the detective, and Chick got together at the O'Neills' to discuss strategy and, mostly, to get a handle on one another.

There was no question that, upon meeting the fire marshal, Margie knew he was one especially annoyed young man. He was black and tough and he was disgusted. His name was Martin Luther King Junior Hightower. Margie said to him, "Nice to meet you, Marshal." He said, "Call me Hightower, ma'am." Even as they sat at the kitchen table organizing who wanted what in their coffee, Hightower immediately made clear exactly what was annoying him: "That circus fire is a dead horse, and I'm not into beating dead horses."

They all looked at him. Actually, they were watching him; he dumped several mounds of sugar into his coffee and a lot of cream. Then he stirred. They kept waiting for his coffee to slosh over the edge of the cup, it was so full. But it didn't. He looked up at them gaping at him. He put down the spoon and he leaned back in his chair. He pointed his finger at the detective. "You're a figurehead here, Mac." The detective's name was not Mac. "Your role is to make this all legal, which it is not. City of Hartford's paying you to waste your time and waste the taxpayers' money." The accusing finger moved in a level line toward Chick, "You . . ." it moved on to Charlie. ". . . and you, are a couple of nutcases. A good cop, a good fireman, but you're both playing with half a deck." He picked up the spoon again, stirred his coffee some more, put the spoon back down, and looked at Margie. He didn't point. "And you, ma'am, you've got an ax to grind."

Margie could understand him thinking that about her, though it wasn't true. Then he said, "And me . . ." (he jabbed his thumb into his chest) ". . . I got better things to do, I'll tell ya. You people are wasting my *valuable* time. But I'm here so let's get it over with."

Though the group had acquiesced to Hightower's stage presence, he couldn't hide his intrigue once Charlie led him into the war room. He took in the blown-up photos and the diagrams and the pictures and the floor-to-ceiling shelves of notebooks, and of course, the wall-sized, bird's-eye view of the tent. In fact, like so many others, he couldn't help but get up and walk over to it. He took the same walk, coffee cup in hand, and made the same gestures as so many of Charlie's witnesses had. But instead of pointing and saying, "I was sitting about here," he pointed and said, "This is where I grew up." He jammed that finger of his into the Map. "Uh, let's see. Grew up in Grandstand B."

He was talking about the final housing project to be built in Hartford, on the site of the last circus tent ever raised in the city. He laughed an especially grating laugh. "My mother still lives there; she's . . . let's see . . . about here . . . on the aisle, tenth row."

He moved along the picture, absorbing it. They watched him the same way they'd watched him stir his coffee, authority and confidence flowing from every gesture. He reminded Margie a lot of Martha. She also thought he reminded her of General Schwarzkopf. But then, so did Martha. He said, talking to the Map, "We can't come up with an arson case against a guy torching a circus fire—let's see—over forty years ago. Statute of limitations. 'Course there's no statute of limitations on murder." He turned and looked at Charlie. "But I know, and I know you two know, . . ." (meaning Chick and the detective) ". . . that arson-murder was not a crime in Connecticut in 1944. You set a fire, someone gets killed, it's an accident. Like when a drunk in his banged-up Chevy mows down a kid on a bike. An accident."

Charlie said, "Intention."

The marshal's laugh was even more harsh than before. "Intention? Arsonists don't set fires to kill people. They do it—excuse me, ma'am—to get their rocks off."

Charlie said, "This one did it to kill people."

Hightower walked over to the table, leaned over it opposite Charlie, and glared into Charlie's face. "You are a joke in the department, man, and you know it. I don't like jokes. I'm too busy. No way anybody's going to prove some guy wanted to kill six thousand people. The guy wanted to watch a burn. He sure as hell got what he wanted. But that's all he wanted. He didn't want to kill kids and tigers and clowns, and nobody in any court of law will prove otherwise."

Charlie, steady as a slab of concrete, said, "If he'd lit the tent half an hour earlier, nobody would have been in it."

"You think you've got premeditation? How many arsonists have you talked to?"

"A few."

"I've talked to a thousand. Maybe more. I spent ten years in New York, where arson is a high-paying job. Arsonists premeditate all right. They watch to make sure no one's in the building. Or else the landlord who hired 'em will dock 'em."

"What about a few years ago? In the Bronx."

"The social club?"

"Yeah."

"That piece of dog turd didn't want to kill anybody. Not his girlfriend, that's for sure. He wanted to impress her is all. And he sure as hell did impress her. Trouble was, he impressed himself while he was at it. Too much of a wimp to think he was capable of killing a cockroach, let alone all those people. He kept saying, 'I didn't kill anybody, sir.' Called everyone sir. 'I just set the fire—that's all I did. I didn't kill anyone. I just set it.' Shit." Hightower stood up straight and rubbed his back. "All arsonists claim the fires are what killed people, not them. Incredible."

The police detective was getting anxious. Margie could see he hadn't bargained for more than just a simple little payback for Chick. Quick trip to Canada and home again. He kept glancing back and forth from Charlie to the fire marshal. Neither Charlie nor Hightower was about to back off. So the police detective finally couldn't take anymore and said, "Well, maybe one of them soldiers on leave took some crackpot's girlfriend to the circus. Pissed him off enough so that he did something . . . uh . . . stupid."

Hightower looked at the detective as if he were seeing more dog turd. The marshal said, "He'd have confessed, or he'd have let himself get caught. If the idea is to impress someone, how do you impress that person if she doesn't know you did it?"

Margie said, "Maybe she died."

He didn't look at Margie like she was dog turd, but he was still pretty disdainful. "Ma'am, there was one person at the social club in the Bronx, New York, that the Cuban goofball made sure was safe—his girlfriend. She was at the doorway when he torched the place. If that's the scenario at the circus, the guy would have waited for the girlfriend to get out of the tent—waited for her to go out and buy a dog, or go to the toilet. An arsonist is not interested in impressing dead people, understand?"

"Yes," Margie said. "Sorry."

He looked into her eyes. "No need to be sorry. What you said made more sense than anything so far." He lifted his shoulders up and down to relieve the tension. They waited for him to keep going. He did. "Listen, friends, we got this psycho up there in Canada we're planning on chitchatting with, and that oughta be rich, believe me. He puts people in sheds and then torches the sheds. But that ain't all he does. They let the pros—me—look further than they let the amateurs—you. This guys hurts his victims first. Hurts them good. He fires them—still alive—one, to cover up what he did, and two, because it's almost as much fun as the other stuff he's done to them already. This guy isn't an arsonist, he's a sociopath. Father was a drunk, his brothers beat him up all the time, and his mother was borderline retarded, same as him."

Charlie said, "Which is why he ran away with the circus. Our circus."

"Yeah. Your circus. So we got a convenient little coincidence here. So what."

"He disappeared after the fire."

"So did everyone else. There was no circus after that fire. Just the top brass who flew in to salvage a real big mess. But the rest of them—they were all out of there as fast as they could get, from the manager to the pack of transients who did the dirty work. Including our boy in Canada. Gone." He snapped his fingers.

Now Hightower came over and sat down. Margie had been wondering if he ever would. He put his empty coffee cup on the table. He was still looking at Charlie. Margie poured him some more coffee. He said, "Thank you, ma'am." He took a few sips. He didn't put in any cream or sugar this time. He said, "Who's got the file?"

The detective had it. Margie had read it already, standing up, as soon as Chick had handed it to her. The file said that Henry Maxson had been confessing to the Hartford circus fire for the last twenty years. But he'd also confessed to kidnapping the Lindbergh baby and to sabotaging the *Hindenburg*, which had taken place before he was born. So the authorities hadn't paid much attention to him. They had enough to do paying attention to finding the bodies of the people he had killed—in culverts, in hollow tree trunks, in deserted houses, in barns and under boardwalks, and in boats, too. Charred bodies, all of them.

Charlie said, "Listen, Hightower. Nobody knew till now that this guy was on the Barnum and Bailey payroll." That was the fact that had grabbed Charlie.

"Besides," Margie chimed in, "even if he didn't do it, he might have seen who did. Charlie's point is, he was there. So

Charlie wants to talk to him. That's what Charlie does."
Margie listened to herself defending the actions she had so
recently attempted to stop.

So now all their eyes swiveled to her. The fire marshal said,
"And you were there, ma'am."

"Yes."

"You make good coffee."

Margie said, "Thanks."

They all sat quietly, drinking their coffee and thinking.
Then Margie said, "I believe the Sox are playing the Blue
Jays this week. Away."

She got four blank stares.

"I checked the atlas. Brampton is a suburb of Toronto."

They kept staring at her while their brains reregistered.
Chick's brain settled in before the others. He said, "How
many games we out?"

The detective said, "Six."

Margie said, "Five in the A.I.L.C."

Hightower said, "What the hell is that?"

Margie said. "The All Important Loss Column. What's the
matter? Don't you like baseball?"

A grin broke out. He roared. He did know how to act
human, Margie was relieved to see.

They flew out to Toronto the next day. Margie noted that
Clemens would be pitching that night—a little bonanza.
Hightower said, "I saw that in the *Courant* this morning."
Margie brought something to read on the plane, the new
paper edition of *Presumed Innocent*. The fire marshal brought a
book, too. The same one as Margie's.

Chapter Fourteen

First the warden showed them a picture of him; it was a photo of a madman. The word *stereotype* came immediately to Margie's mind. But in addition to his wild eyes and an Albert Einstein shock of hair, he was scarred. His arms and his face were almost all scar tissue, and the gaps in his hair showed shiny white patches. The warden said, "Whenever he gets near a match, near a stove, near anything that burns, he tries to set fire to himself."

Margie said, "Don't you have hospitals for people like that in this country?"

The warden said, "You're in it. Hospitals for the criminally insane are also called prisons."

The warden had led them through a series of locked doors, through a maze of corridors, and down flights of damp staircases, and Margie figured they were at least three floors below ground when the warden said, "He's just down this hall."

Hall is not what Margie would have called the grim and dirty cement tunnel they were in, the echoes of their footfalls a lot louder than the footfalls themselves. Margie whispered to Charlie, "You know who else is in this basement, don't you?"

The Hartford detective heard her. He said, "Who?"

Charlie whispered, "Hannibal Lecter." He'd seen the video.

The detective said, "Who's he?"

The fire marshal smiled. He whispered, "Not to worry. He's in Rio."

Margie said to Charlie, "I *told* you it was Rio. It just *looked* like Jamaica." She said to Hightower, "You read the book, right?"

He said, "I only read the book."

No wonder I like him, Margie thought.

Chick said, "Can it, you guys."

When death has been a major part of your day-to-day living, you develop a sick sense of humor. Like Kurt Vonnegut, Margie thought. Chick put the hobbles on them because the warden kept eyeing them—the way they were whispering and giggling, their nerves jangled. Hightower and Margie had become conspirators, suddenly, and she was wired. Hightower composed himself. He said to the warden, "Frankly, I've never heard of an arsonist who likes to set fire to himself."

The warden said, "Count your blessings. Wish I never heard of any."

Henry Maxson was in a lounge. It wasn't really a lounge; it was some sort of all-purpose room. Nonpurpose room was what Margie thought. Now it had been cleared out for people needing a meeting. The walls were cement block, unpainted, the floor was cement, too, and there were chairs and a table with a phone. The phone didn't have any sort of dialing mechanism. Henry Maxson was handcuffed, wrists and ankles, to a chair. A state psychiatrist was in another chair. The warden said, "This is Dr. Glass." Dr. Glass nodded. Everyone nodded back, including Henry Maxson. The warden didn't introduce anyone to Henry Maxson. Instead, the warden said to him, "Well, Henry, here are the people I told you about."

Henry remained relaxed, except that Margie could see the tendons sticking up from his wrists. He was exerting tension on his wrist and ankle restraints, but managed to make the rest of his body slack. Once when Margie had gone to a La Leche League meeting, hoping someone would be able to show her how to go about breast-feeding, a woman was there who said that when her baby took the breast, the first few seconds of sucking hurt her nipples. The La Leche leader said to treat her tender nipples with ice, but until her nipples toughened up she should grit her teeth, grip the armrest of her chair with her free hand, and relax the rest of her body so the baby wouldn't feel the tension. Until this day at the Canadian prison, Margie couldn't see how a person could possibly manage such a feat. Or why. You can't protect babies from tension, anyway. But Henry needed to hide his tension so they'd believe whatever it was he intended to say.

There were two empty chairs facing Henry, and three in a row behind those two, and then two more behind them. Margie was reminded of the flight deck of the *Challenger*. The shrink was in the last row. She took the chair next to him. She thought: Christa McAuliffe's. The warden and Charlie sat up front, and Chick, the detective, and Hightower were in the middle. Charlie opened the briefcase he was carrying. He unrolled a miniversion of the Map, reached over, and laid it across Henry's lap. Henry didn't look down at it. Instead, his eyes took in everyone assembled in front of him, and he said, "The devil come riding on his red horse that day. The devil come riding." He paused. He spoke like a third-grader reciting the lines of some mediocre poem deemed suitable for children to memorize. Then he said, shifting his face toward Margie, "When the devil come on his red horse, I gotta set a fire."

The psychiatrist said, "He's talking about masturbation."

The men turned to look at the psychiatrist. Margie just glanced toward him, but then went right back to Henry. She was mesmerized by Henry Maxson. The psychiatrist continued in his monotone, "When he masturbates he is usually unable to ejaculate, so when he becomes aroused, he looks for something to kill. His first choice is a female, young or old, he doesn't care. But he kills men and boys, too. He kills each victim by setting them on fire. Foreplay consists of torturing them—well, usually *her*—first. Then he's able to ejaculate while he watches, and of course listens, to the begging and pleading, and finally the screaming. In the cases of animals he's burned, I don't know what he's listening for."

The men looked back to Henry. The whites of his eyes were red. Margie wondered what they had him on. Henry said very quietly, "I only kill people that are happy."

Charlie, calm as stone, said, "Why is that?"

Henry said, "Because I didn't ever know a happy day in my life."

The psychiatrist cleared his throat. Everyone looked back to him except Margie and Henry. "His father and brothers would take turns beating him at night. They'd hit him every time he managed to fall asleep. Actually, the father forced the brothers to help. A child tortured in his sleep—so that he *can't* sleep—is a human being in such torment that there is simply no telling what that torment will lead to."

Margie felt her stomach turn over. Henry's eyes changed a little bit as he saw the reflection of her distress in her face. Charlie said to him, "Why did you set the tent on fire?"

Henry said, like a person scornfully addressing someone he

considered a dumbbell, "Because the people inside were happy."

The psychiatrist's turn, in his same calm voice: "What it comes down to is that he wants us to believe that he was trying to kill his father. That's what the social workers keep telling him. Now he's beginning to think that if he goes along with that, he'll get out of here. Get out of here so he can get his hands on some matches.

"He's killed at least fifty people by my count. A few animals. Four dogs, as a matter of fact, and cats. Lots of cats. He burned all of them alive. When he got the fire going, he'd masturbate to the sight and sound of their suffering. He became so adept at . . . it, that he'd hold his ejaculation to what he calculated to be the final scream."

Margie was still looking into Henry's eyes, he into hers. Then his ravaged lips turned up. He was smiling at her. Charlie's head turned slightly back, and though he didn't take his own eyes off Henry, he spoke carefully to Margie. "Leave the room." The others were confused. Margie wasn't. Henry wasn't. She got up and went to the door, Henry's eyes touching her back like a hand, leaving his thumbprint.

Two guards were just outside. Margie asked to be taken to a bathroom. Another guard had to come to take her with him and by the time she got to a bathroom she had willed away throwing up. She said to the guard, "I want to go back. Can I listen to them without going into the room?"

He said, "Sure."

When they got back Margie sat down by a narrow slit in the wall. She could see Henry's profile. She sat down just in time to hear Henry say, "Because I seen someone set it."

She thought, damn! She'd missed something big. Henry was reneging. Maybe what Henry was trying to do now was simple—if he testified that someone else had set the fire, he'd still have a chance of convincing them to let him out, get his hands on some matches. Margie waited for Charlie to speak. Finally, Charlie asked, "Who set it?"

Henry said, "A kid."

"What kid?"

"A little kid. He sat down right behind the tent . . . over here." His profile turned downward. He was looking at the Map, pointing, kind of, with his chin. "Behind Grandstand A. Nobody back there. Just me. I didn't have nothing to do till it was time for intermission. Then I'm supposed to help at the food stands. When the animal act gets finished up, the animals need a lot of attention, so the roustabouts, they were all on the other side of the chute over by the wagons, along the side of the wagons in case some animal got stubborn and wouldn't move. Or got stuck between 'em. Sometimes that happened.

"The kid didn't see me. He twisted up a bunch of newspapers, lit 'em, and held 'em up against the canvas. A wind came up and blew some of the paper outa his hands. The pieces hit the tent and it caught. About eight feet up. Then the kid ran away. I watched the tent burn. Then I ran away, too. I knew they'd blame me for it. I got blamed for everything, especially shit I didn't do."

No one said anything, so Henry said to Charlie, "That your wife was in here before?"

Charlie stood up and took the Map off Henry's lap. He headed for the door but he wasn't fast enough. Henry said, "I would burn her cunt first."

Margie knew he'd say something like that. The guy who wrote *The Silence of the Lambs* knew what this business was all about. She was beginning to wonder if maybe the author had interviewed Henry. Even though Charlie tried to get out before Henry spoke, the others weren't expecting he'd say what he said, and they were still sitting, stricken. Henry saw to it that they'd hear, once he realized that he was not going to get out. Henry planned it. Margie knew he was planning it. The words themselves meant nothing to Henry; but Margie suspected he got the reaction he was looking for.

Nobody could look at Margie when they left the room. Except the psychiatrist. He said to Margie, "He was a terribly abused child."

Margie said, "I know. That's why this isn't really bothering me."

That night at SkyDome, Margie realized what a pretty song the Canadian national anthem was. Even though it took "Oh Canada" to make her feel she was back in the real world again, she couldn't get into the game and neither could anyone else. They'd glance up when a roar rose from the crowd, glance up whenever the new guy stepped up to the plate—the big black rookie from Connecticut—glance up at each of Clemens's pitches, all the while talking and cracking peanuts. They shelled bag after bag of peanuts, eating them the way chain-smokers devour cigarettes. They took turns going for beer. As soon as the beer person came back, he'd say, "What'd I miss?" just like at a normal ball game. But he wasn't talking about the game. He was referring to the Henry Maxson debate. It took them six innings to stop discussing Henry Maxson and his version of the story; the kid he saw set the fire. It was Hightower who couldn't take any more, who just got tired of trying to convince them what he believed about Henry Maxson. So he changed tack. He became philosophical instead as he tried to get across what he felt one last time.

He sat back into his seat, looked out at the game, and said, "I do my job. That's all I've ever wanted to do. Just my job. When there's a fire in Hartford, some black family or some 'Rican family—sometimes even some white family—they don't have a place to live anymore. That's why I know where you're comin' from, Charlie. I want to catch the firebugs so they don't set more fires. So two old people won't be out on the street without even a photograph to remember their lives before they get shuffled off to somewhere they don't want to go. But here, you and me split off. This guy Maxson set that fire. I know it. You know it. He was describing himself, telling us how he did it. And he's caught. He's not going to get out of there because this isn't a book where the bad guy escapes by eating the face off a dumb guard and then ends up in Rio. No more fires from Henry Maxson. So what's your point, Charlie? Why is it that I'm satisfied and you're not?"

Charlie said nothing. That's because he didn't think that Henry Maxson did it. He believed that what Henry Maxson said was true. Hightower had no idea that Charlie didn't believe that Henry Maxson had been describing himself. Chick knew and Margie knew, and her pain at having to face the fact that Charlie's search was about something else— something she couldn't grasp—was almost as difficult as coming to terms with the fact that Chick must have known what that something else was. If not, why didn't Palma tell *him* to get Charlie to stop? He was supposed to be Charlie's protector.

The fire marshal was oblivious to all the family machinations he knew nothing about, and he just went on philosophizing. "You're right, Charlie. You've been right all along. Barnum and Bailey was arson. Some psychotic tried to kill six thousand people, and we just got to meet him, lucky us. Henry Maxson tried to kill them because his brand of arson wasn't about impressing anyone. It was about raping his father, I guess. Or his mother, who stood by. Destroying people's happiness the way his had been destroyed. I guess.

"But shit, so what? The thing is, he's been found, and he can't kill anybody else. The point isn't even that; the point is that we've got laws on the books now that weren't there before. So does the circus. Circus tents today couldn't burn if you held a blowtorch to them. It's not going to happen anymore. Isn't that justice, Charlie? Isn't what we just witnessed what you've been looking for?"

Margie's instinct was to jump in and make an excuse for Charlie. But she had to stop doing that. She knew she had to stop if she really wanted to figure out just what it was that made Charlie the brand of angry that he was. She had to decide to love him or not love him, for better or worse. She wasn't his mother; she had a choice here, so she just sat back and gripped the arms of her seat to hide the tension she felt. She just set herself like concrete and listened to Charlie say, "I don't know it."

"You don't know what?"

"That Maxson did it. I'm going to find the kid he saw do it. The same kid Dixie saw."

First, there was just the noise of the game. A lot of noise. Someone must have made a great play. Then the detective said, "Who the hell is Dixie?" Margie looked at Hightower staring at Charlie, but Hightower wasn't really surprised like the detective was. He recognized a brick wall when he saw one. So he stayed philosophical, though his philosophy grew an edge.

"White people are fools. They strive. And they keep striving even after there's nothing left to strive for. They watch 'Lifestyles of the Rich and Famous' on TV, and figure there's more. There ain't. They could have all the money in the world and they'll keep trying to get more. Never fucking satisfied. Sorry, ma'am.

"Strive for something else, O'Neill, if you don't know how to stop. For something worthwhile. Worth your while and everyone else's, too. Keep fighting fires. More of them. Perfect job for a white boy because the fires ain't never going to go out."

Charlie said, "That's right. That's what I'm going to keep doing. But meantime, I'm not going to quit on this fire. Soon as I finish striving for this, maybe I'll just be able to concentrate on tomorrow's fire. Maybe I'll strive for not finding any more little girls at the bottom of their closets hugging their teddy bears, burned and dead. But all I know is somebody's going to pay for all the little girls burned in that circus."

Margie held on to her seat. Charlie was Charlie. He'd never find who set the circus fire because searching for him was part of his character, just like the fire was part of the city's character. This was Charlie's reason for being, just the way her father claimed his wife was his only reason for being. Charlie would be as dead as her father had been in that room in the veterans' home if he stopped trying to find the person who set the fire, even though he'd just found him. That was it. Period. Charlie would never believe Henry did it, not because of what the animal trainer's assistant had said almost twenty years ago, but because he plain didn't want to, and why he didn't want to was what would keep him striving. And why he didn't want to was why Margie was going to leave him.

She really did love him, she knew, but there was no changing Charlie. She'd *have* to leave him. Her role as a crutch was over. He didn't need a crutch to do what he was doing. Not anymore. That's what his mother saw. Get him to stop, she told Margie. Margie wondered if Palma's words were advice—that she should threaten to leave him so that he'd stop. If that's what she meant, she was wrong. Nothing would stop him. But Margie would have to leave him to get the resentment that was overwhelming her to desist.

People told Margie her father used to wear immaculate white spats when he courted her mother. Ever since she could remember, her father hadn't cared what he was wearing.

Margie looked over at Charlie. He had a nice profile. Henry Maxson's profile was lumpy and unnatural. Charlie's had those soft eyelashes. Henry had no eyelashes left. Margie wanted to shake Charlie and scream at him: Henry did it, Henry did it—Henry killed my mother! Henry's threat to burn me hurt you because he already did burn me. And now you can't get your revenge.

But she didn't scream anything. It would do no good. She would leave him instead. She could do it, but she'd have to call Martha first for help.

Chapter Fifteen

Margie and Martha met in New York at a sushi bar halfway between Grand Central and Penn stations. Martha had taken the Metroliner from Washington, where she was a law student at Georgetown. She had a bag of work with her that she'd gotten done on the train. Margie had read a book on the train from Hartford. They had a nice cozy booth and started with Kirin beer on empty stomachs. With all the catching up that went on, they had another beer before the sushi came. And a third with the sushi, which was when they got down to business.

Martha hiccoughed when she said, "Mom, I love Dad."

"I know you do."

"So it's difficult to be objective."

"I know that, too."

"And Dad loves me. He loves us. He would never hurt us. He would never hurt you."

"I know."

"I'm telling you all these things you already know to get warmed up. So stop saying 'I know.'"

"Okay."

"I'm saying all these things so that I can say what you haven't thought about, even though you probably know it."

"Know what?"

"Listen, Mom. Because of those two things—because he really does love you and because he'd die before he'd hurt you—because of that, you can feel free to leave him."

Martha meant to know the law, the unwritten as well as the written, and she also had decided to cut right to the charge and give her mother the truth. She said, "Even when the truth is a relief, it still hurts." Margie wondered how her daughter's generation figured these things out before they grew up. Where did they find them out? Who told them?

Margie said, "You'd have never made it in L'Aquila."

"Where?"

"Where honor is better than coping."

"Honor is a way of coping."

"What are we talking about?"

"Dad. We're talking about Dad. You're worried about his coping with what you have to do. Naturally, he'll feel bad."

"He'll feel real bad, sweetie."

"But not nearly as bad as you're feeling right now."

Yeah. Margie dipped a piece of raw fish into soy sauce and ate it. Her Uncle Pete used to scoop oysters out of the creek at Chalker Beach with a crab net. He'd open them with a jackknife, then they'd look for pearls, and then he, Little Pete, and Margie would eat them. They'd had to promise not to tell Aunt Jane. "Martha, why would a woman leave a man who loves her?"

Martha went into discourse as she wielded her chopsticks

like she'd been born holding them. And who the hell taught her that? "There's just one reason a woman leaves a man who loves her. Or who doesn't love her, for that matter. Because she doesn't love *him*." Martha paused, but then changed her mind. She wouldn't give her mother a chance to say something about Italians. "That's not to say she didn't once love him. A whole lot, even." She practically swallowed a shrimp whole.

"Chew, Martha!"

"I'm chewing. You don't owe somebody just because he loves you. Since love should never be demanding—I learned that in a class about Hindu philosophy"—Margie thought, Yale!—"there's no need to feel that you owe someone. Now I know that's not what you believe, not being a Hindi, but we're talking here about owing someone your whole life. See, sometimes the picture gets too big, and you can't see a damn thing."

Then Martha was the second person after Palma to say the word *divorce*. Martha went ahead and slipped it in. "I'll tell you, Mom, it's really incredibly fascinating when couples are getting divorced. If a man loves a woman who doesn't love him anymore, he fights to make her love him. He'll berate her, bully her, or keep telling her how much he's done for her, or accuse her of being out of her mind, and he just won't give up until she comes back to him, or until she's no longer there, at which time he goes on berating anyone who will listen. Of course, if she does give in, and comes back— defeated, I'd have to call it, or maybe exhausted—he'll insist everything's just fine again, and think he's wonderful for keeping the marriage together. Men think that if a woman isn't yelling and screaming, she's happy as a clam. So on top of not loving him anymore the woman who goes back loses all respect for her husband because he's so content to be happy with an empty marriage."

"That's not how Dad would act."

"Mom, I'm just giving you the average scenario so you'll have something to compare your own to. So listen, when the woman is tough, and leaves, the husband always needs so much help. Those guys are pathetic. But guess what?"

"What?"

"The unhappy, suicide-talking little fellas marry someone else before a year's up. It's easy to find another woman to berate, apparently.

'But Mom, when it's the other way around—when the man leaves—when a woman still loves a man who doesn't love her anymore, she'll be just as kind and as sweet as she can be, figuring if she acts like a good girl, he'll realize how wonderful she is and take her back. And let me tell you, if you're a lawyer, that translates to a refusal on the wife's part to fight for what belongs to her. So not only does she end up with no husband, she ends up destitute. So now she comes back to her lawyer, a year later, too late, naturally. She's trying to pay for home and hearth while her ex-husband is at the Guadaloupe Club Med with some bimbo. She still can't understand why he went through with the divorce—after all, she'd been so nice—but now it hits her that he's also completely ripped her off. She's there with all the bills and he's got his C-card—too stupid to know that he's not young enough to be a yuppie."

"What's a C-card?"

"Certification to have your tanks filled."

"What tanks?"

Martha laughed. "I'm teasing you, Ma. Scuba tanks."

"Oh."

"You can never trust a man with a C-card. He spends more time blow-drying his hair than you do."

"I can't imagine Jacques Cousteau blow-drying his hair."

"We're not talking about *real* divers, here, Ma."

"What *are* we talking about?"

"Something that hurts too much to talk about." Martha

sighed. "Where's the waiter?" Two more beers arrived, the waiter only a second behind them for this next round. "Mom, you and Dad aren't a couple of jerks. Maybe I'm telling you about the typical divorce so that you'll know that . . . so you'll know that . . . Oh, shit, I don't know."

Margie watched her daughter struggle not to be stern. Margie said, "You know so much, baby. You really do."

"No, I don't." Martha wiped a finger across her empty plate and licked off the soy-sauce drippings. "It's just that I've got this streak of blarney I must have inherited from that famous shit of all times, my evil Irish grandfather."

"God I wish that man had died a hell of a lot sooner."

"At Dad's birth, for example?"

"Exactly."

"You blame him for Dad's obsession?"

"Yes. I blame him for abusing your father and his other children. If emotional abuse is what led to Dad's obsession, then that's what I blame him for."

"Why do you suppose Uncle Mike and Uncle Frank aren't obsessive?"

"Martha, is obsession what we're dealing with here? Dad's not really obsessive. I mean, he certainly isn't about anything else."

"I suppose. But then again, how would we know that? He doesn't do anything else."

"Yes he does. He does what men do. He watches TV, he goes to firemen parties, he reads the paper, we go see a movie."

Martha sighed again. "Well, let's face it, Mom. Maybe you're just bored."

"Why would you say such a thing, Martha?"

"I'm sorry. I got frustrated with you."

"You're never bored when you're with someone you love. Sometimes I sit and just watch him watch TV. He's a good person. He's good to me. He's always been good to you."

"I know that. But so what? What's that got to do with what we're here for? You've gone along with his very weird behavior and you don't want to do that anymore. No more denial, Ma. Let's deal with that instead of love."

"Deal with the hurting part?"

"That's right. You've changed into a different person than what you were when you first got married. You feel like starting up again—trying something different. There's just nothing you can do about the fact that he isn't." Martha picked up her beer glass and put it down again. "I need tea." The pot arrived. She said to her mother, "Of course, you could talk to him."

Margie poured her own tea. Martha's attempt had left more tea on the table than in her cup. Margie did no better. "Believe it or not, I have talked to him. A little. I'm not going to change him. But Martha, the obsession thing was part of him when I met him. I married him for better or worse. How could I change my mind about the worse part?"

"You can change your mind because you'd just turned eighteen when you made that ridiculous promise. You didn't know what worse might be. You couldn't predict how you'd be when you grew up. People change. People need to renegotiate their marriage every few years."

"What's that? The party line?"

"Yeah." She grinned. That grin in court would someday put juries in her back pocket. Margie didn't say that, though.

"Want some more tea, Martha?"

Martha's grin dissolved. "Why now, Mom?" She waited a little longer than usual to see if Margie would respond. She knew her mother would need time. So after a few moments, Margie filled in the pause.

"Martha, Miss Foss was right. She just didn't use the right words on me."

Martha said, "Miss *who*?"

"My high school guidance counselor. I didn't go to college because she didn't tell me the truth. She was mean-spirited."

"What was the truth?"

"That I was already smart enough to know that the horse-radish was no place to be. That the problem was that I wouldn't admit it."

"Jesus, Mom, fill in, okay?"

Margie filled in. Then she said, "She could have helped me face the truth."

"Miss Foss was probably the only counselor for the senior class."

"No. For all the girls at Hartford High."

"Then she didn't have time. That and the fact that she was frustrated with you. So she had to hand you the party line."

"Martha, what do you think educated people end up with that I don't have?"

Martha thought. She had no ready answer this time. Then she said, "My friends who didn't go to college stayed eighteen. They stopped in their tracks. Not going to college is a safety net. You get to stay a kid. You get to be lazy; you don't have to think anymore. It's a crutch, not being educated. If you go and make a mistake in your life, everyone will say, 'What did she know? She got married right out of high school.' The more you learn, the more mature you're expected to act."

"Is that what happened to me, then? To my life?"

"Yes, that's what happened. But it's not necessarily a permanent condition." She waited. Margie said nothing. "Mom, your batteries are charging up. Probably because your life is half over. You want the second half to be different. Happens all the time. The chief cause of divorce in the middle-aged."

"But Martha, I'm not completely uneducated. I read so much. I read all the time. I love to read. I've learned a lot."

"You read for entertainment. *War and Peace* is not the same as your kill-the-baby books."

"*When the Bough Breaks,* you mean?"

Martha laughed at her mother. "Exactly. Actually, I envy you. You've got the right attitude. I'll bet Tolstoy just wanted to entertain us."

"Martha, I want to stay serious."

"Sorry. Listen, Mom, do you ever think about what an author is trying to say to you about human nature?"

"I didn't think authors were trying to tell me anything about human nature."

"Oh, Mom."

"Wait. Yes, I did. Once. I went to see *Who's Afraid of Virginia Woolf?* I wrote to the playwright. I asked him if the play meant that God was dead. If George, the history professor, ate the telegram that said the son was dead as a way to show the audience that the evidence was swallowed up by history. The son being the son of God. So that nobody could really *prove* whether God was dead or not." Margie grew animated. She loved to storytell. It had been a long time. "Then there were these two other characters in the play—a science teacher and his dumb little wife. And I figured the dumb little wife was someone like me, and that she wanted to have a baby and couldn't so she put her faith in her husband instead of God—the husband being science. Well, anyway, he wrote back and told me I was the only one who got his message."

"Who wrote back?"

"Martha. The playwright."

"Tommy Agee wrote you a letter?"

"Jesus, Martha. Tommy Agee was a baseball player. *Edward Albee* is the playwright."

Then Margie laughed. They both laughed. So much beer. Margie said, "I get it, Martha. All those baseball games we took you to. You never analyzed them, did you?"

"No."

"But you enjoyed them."

"Still do."

"What does ERA stand for?"

Martha's lips parted, she stopped herself, she smiled, and then she let herself say, "Equal Rights Amendment."

Now they became hysterical. They laughed until they wept. The sushi chef behind the bar laughed, too. Martha did not point out to her mother that this was the first time she'd heard her laugh out loud. Martha said, "I have a confession to make."

"What?"

"I don't know what 'base on balls' means."

"What?"

"I said, I don't know what 'base on balls' means."

"Of course you do. You're making a point, right?"

"I'm not! I mean, I'm making a point, but I still don't know what 'base on balls' means."

"It's obvious what 'base on balls' means."

"Not if you don't feel like figuring it out. Not if you just want the romance of baseball without all the gobbledygook."

"Martha! I demand that you think and figure out what 'base on balls' means."

A plaintive look came over Martha's face. "Please don't make me. My head hurts. Just tell me, Mom, okay?"

"A base on balls is a walk."

"Oh. Oh, yeah. But then, shouldn't it be: 'base on four balls'?"

"That would be redundant."

They started to laugh all over again, and then Martha reached over and took both her mother's hands. She said, "Once in an American Lit class, the final exam was the question, 'Why was Moby Dick white?' And I thought, If my mother were here she'd write that Moby Dick's father was white and his mother was white, too, that's why he's white. And then she'd walk out of the room."

"See? I *wasn't* college material. That's exactly what I would have done." Margie looked down at their four hands. Then she looked back up at Martha. "I wanted more children than just you. I let him do everything his way. A woman will do anything for a man if he's nice to her. Boys were never nice to me. They patronized me, which wasn't the same thing."

Martha had used up her tears laughing, so there was none that formed now. She said, "Oh, Mommy."

"And I let him think everything, too. But now *I* want to do the thinking. As soon as I figure out what it is I want to do, I'll do it. But it's too damn late, isn't it? It *is* too late. What will I do?"

Martha had no answer for her mother, so she had to go with a brief. "Of course it isn't too late. Find a route. If you look for one, you'll find one. If we have to switch the parent-child roles around for a while, I don't mind. I'll take care of both of you while it happens. And Mom?"

"What, sweetheart?"

"I'm glad you didn't have other children. I'd have had to share all the love."

Chapter Sixteen

After Martha, Margie went to talk to Chick. She wanted to see him alone, too. That meant more beer. She met him at Jack Potter's old haunt, the Brookside Tavern. First, all the patrons told Margie how sorry they were to hear about her Dad. She enjoyed talking about him and thanking the old men for being his friend when he'd needed them, though she didn't note that it was only two times a year. Then Chick came in and he and Margie sipped their beers and chatted until he said to her, "You ready to spill the beans yet, kiddo?"

She was. "How come no one ever told me that Aunt Annette and the girls were at the circus? And besides that, I'm wondering what else no one's ever told me."

"It was a slip."

"Which?"

"The first thing."

"And the second?"

"No one's ever kept anything from you, Margie."

"You're lying on both counts."

"Martha's been in town."

"Yeah, but we talked baseball."

"That must have been rich."

"She said she likes Mike Greenwell better without the mustache." Margie put down her beer so she could keep to what she was there for. "Uncle Chick, I thought you and Charlie had some sort of genes thing. An ethnic Italian thing. Or some mental problem with psychopathic compulsion mixed in. But you don't. He does, you don't. There's more going on that nobody's ever let me see, a lot more."

Chick put his arm around her shoulders. "Margie," he said, "Charlie's father was a piece of shit."

"Jesus, that's the one thing I do know. I was fortunate enough to have met him, remember?"

"Yeah. I remember."

"So what's that got to do with what I'm saying?"

"Charlie took it the hardest."

"Took what the hardest? His father's being a shit?"

"His father's abuse."

"Emotional abuse."

"Yes." But then Chick sighed, and that made Margie cringe, but she kept on.

Margie said, "He took it harder than his brothers took it?"

"No. His father gave it to him the hardest. Charlie took the brunt."

Margie knew that "took the brunt" wasn't metaphor. The time had come for her to go past that. Past the term *emotional abuse*, which had become her catch-all term for all the denial going on in her husband's family. She'd never wanted to go forward. She'd been too afraid of what she'd find. The fact that she never wanted to hear had given Charlie's family great relief. And she had used that relief as an excuse. But what she had given Charlie was the crutch of all crutches. No more. Margie wasn't going to go through the rest of her life without finding out what base on balls meant.

Chick drained his beer. While he chugged, Margie said, "Palma told me you protected Charlie from his father. So tell me; just what exactly did Denny try to do to Charlie that you had to protect him from?" She used the same tone as if she was asking him what he'd had for dinner.

"Palma told you the truth. The old man never laid a hand on those kids because of me and my brothers."

"What did he do to them instead?"

His chin dropped to his chest. Looking down into his empty glass, he said, "Imagine owing your life to someone who hated you. Imagine that it's your father. Imagine that your father wanted nothing more than to hurt and hurt and hurt your mother. And the best way he could hurt her was to terrorize you. What the old man did to Charlie, over and over again, was hand him a lollipop. And when Charlie went to put the lollipop in his mouth, his old man yanked it away. To make Palma suffer agonies."

"Uncle Chick," Margie said, "that's real pretty. But would you forget the lollipops. Could you make it as unpretty as possible so I can stay with this?"

"I saw him trip Charlie once."

Chick rubbed his eyes with his thumb and fingers. Margie's stomach was beginning to get an empty pit feeling, even though it was half full of Coors. She would have to bear it. So she waited. Chick said, "The kid was about two. Running around with all the other kids at the park. On the basketball court. The big ones were teaching the little ones. The old man put his foot out. We all ran to pick up Charlie. He was bleeding. His nose, his knees. You know how kids bleed when they fall on their faces."

Margie was going to say yeah, but nothing would come out.

"Through the blood, Charlie stared at his old man. The old man was standing a few feet away, smiling at him."

He stopped telling Margie.

Rage filled up the rest of her stomach. But her rage was not directed at Charlie's father—not toward the man whose name Chick could not even bring himself to say out loud. And she had no rage for Chick either because Margie guessed that that was probably the last time Denny O'Neill physically hurt his son. The rage was toward someone she never expected to feel even a bit of anger toward. Margie said, "And where the hell was Palma? Where was she when her husband was tripping his baby? *Her* baby. Where was she while she suffered her agonies? At home eating? Telling herself that her brothers would never let her husband lay a finger on him? Or was she there?"

The chin went up. "Palma loved her kids."

"Yeah, well, don't we all? But where was she when all the kids were playing and Denny O'Neill tripped their two-year-old onto a basketball court? Made of poured concrete like most basketball courts, I suppose. Where was she when he made her baby bleed?"

"He was like that to everyone, not just Charlie."

"Sorry, but Charlie took the brunt of it, remember? Where was Palma when Denny tripped Charlie?"

"I can't remember."

"Jesus Christ. She was there, goddamn it. She was right there!"

Now Chick shouted. "If she wasn't there, he wouldn't have done it."

"Oh, my God."

"Margie! What the hell's the matter with you?"

"*Charlie* is what's the matter with me. *Charlie*. He'll never be okay, Chick. Never. Let's get him out. He's going to snap, you know. I can see it. So we have to start somewhere. With Palma."

"And what the fuck good would that do?" He caught himself. "Margie, I'm so sorry."

"Chick, tell me more. Tell me everything."

"I shoved him down a flight of stairs."

"What?"

"Right afterward. I shoved the old man down the cellar stairs. Down to the concrete. So he'd know I saw. Broke his wrist. I was hoping he'd break his leg so he wouldn't trip anyone for a while."

"Why didn't you hope he'd break his neck?"

"Murder two."

This would not become a joke. Margie raised her voice. "And why didn't you admit to yourself that it didn't work? That it didn't stop him? That he kept right on tripping that child?"

"He didn't."

"Psychologically."

"He knew that I respected my sister. He wouldn't cross the line."

Cross the line. Code time. Familial codes that were becoming more and more repugnant to Margie. But she was not at the bar with Chick to fight him. She said, "Charlie's father took his circus ticket from him."

"Yes."

"You know, when I first met Charlie, he told me he had a ticket to the circus. I thought it was a joke. Why did he want me to think that?"

"Because he didn't want you to know his pain. I mean, what with yours. Margie, I dropped them off at the bus stop that day. Couldn't take them myself because I was going on duty. Charlie was about to bust, he was so excited so see the circus. But the old man came along, took the ticket, and sent Charlie home. I've decided that God works in mysterious ways."

"God saved him from the fire so that his father could kill him slowly?"

"His father maybe saved his life, Margie."

"No. If his life was saved, it was saved through extenuating circumstances—the bad luck of being an abused child."

"All comes out in the wash though, doesn't it?"

"You just keep right on telling yourself that, Uncle Chick. You and your whole goddamn family."

Then Chick took Margie in his arms and held her because she started crying. She'd cried more in the last few days than she had in all her life. Except when she was six months old.

Margie went home. Maybe she'd find hope there, amongst all her books, surrounded by pages with comforting stories that weren't real.

Charlie got off at eleven and when he came home, he made an omelette for them. The whole Hartford Fire Department makes great omelettes. With provolone cheese. While they were eating the omelette, Margie couldn't help herself. She said, "Charlie, I want to be your psychiatrist."

He said, "That's what you've been."

"I think I've been your drug."

"What's that supposed to mean?"

"You depend on me the way your father depended on alcohol."

He turned, faced her, handed Margie a knife, and opened his shirt. He said, "You want to slash me a little deeper?"

Charlie was not the kind of idiot who made gestures like that, who'd say stupid things like that. She apologized. For herself and for him. Then she said, "I want to know what's inside your head. I need to know, Charlie, why you've had to do this circus stuff. For all this time."

"I don't have any secrets. The reasons are simple. Sometimes, Margie, reasons can be just plain simple."

His soothing answers would not work with her anymore. "We like to think that, Charlie, but the thing is, what you're saying is just not true."

"You used to admire me for what I'm saying. Now you tell me I've been lying to you for twenty-five years."

"I admire you for so much. I still do. But now I know there's more than what I used to think. But listen. Maybe it really is simple—a different kind of simple. Like revenge."

"Okay. Revenge, too."

"Revenge for what?"

His face became full of the need to speak. He didn't.

"Charlie, tell me what you're feeling right now."

"I don't know what I'm feeling."

"Yes, you do. Say it."

"Panic."

"You're feeling panic right now?"

"Yes."

"Tell me what panic is. I've never felt it."

His face changed. To astonishment. Charlie was astonished that panic wasn't a common, everyday feeling. He said, "It's the feeling you get when you're a small kid, and an adult is going to hurt you and there's no escaping."

Some kind of little moan came out of Margie. She swallowed. She said, "I'm sorry I'm making you feel like that. What did he do to you?"

"No, Margie."

"Go ahead, Charlie. Tell me. No adult ever tried to hurt me when I was a kid. I don't know anything about not being able to escape. Tell me."

"I love you."

"I love you, too. Go ahead."

"He didn't hurt me."

"What did he do then?"

"He'd grab hold of my wrist, pull me up to his face, and say: 'You're a fucking little shit, and I hope you get hit by a Mack truck.' "

Tears sprang into Margie's eyes. She said, "How old were you?"

He looked away. Out of frustration. She wasn't getting it. They both could see that. So he tried again. "Margie, I was every age. That was the just the refrain. He said other things, things like that, all the time, every day, just loud enough for my mother to hear. Then he'd say to her, 'Come on over here and give me a kiss.'"

"But she wouldn't." Margie's voice was sharp.

"Of course she would. If she didn't, what would he do to me next?"

Margie took his hand and hung on. She hadn't wanted to touch him before in order to tough it out. She'd tried to do it alone. But she needed him. And all she could say was, "I don't understand."

"You'd never understand. You weren't there."

"That's right." Margie pulled away because she would get too weak. "I wasn't. So you have to tell me more. Tell me about your mother."

"My mother was a saint."

Margie looked up into his eyes. She could not let herself respond, but there was no choice. She forced herself to speak. She said, "Come into the living room with me."

He did. He didn't ask why. He followed her. He thrived on the trust he had in her. His melodramatic comment about her slashing him reflected a sudden loss of trust. Now he was in that panic he'd described. She was going to hurt him, and he couldn't escape. Margie wished she were dead.

In the living room there was a little Victorian mirror in a corner. Margie put Charlie in front of it. She said, "Look at you, Charlie. You're not a kid anymore. Your father can't hurt you anymore. You're a grown man. A strong man." She was rambling, but if she took time to think of what she was saying, she'd stop.

"You can take the truth. You have no choice, anyway. Because I'm not going to let you have a choice anymore. Face up to your mother. Get pissed at her. That's what you need to do. She wasn't a saint, she was in a trap like you were. But she was an adult, not a child. Get pissed at her. For keeping you in that trap with her. Get pissed at all this shit about Chick protecting you. He didn't protect you, did he? *Did he? Did he?"*

Charlie smashed his fist into the mirror. Margie had never seen Charlie so much as swat a fly before. She'd never seen him cry, either. First he punched the mirror with his fist, and then he started sobbing.

Margie ran to the phone. Dr. Spinelli, their family doctor, took care of lots of kids so he was used to being woken up at midnight. Later, as he picked the glass out of Charlie's knuckles with his tweezers, he looked up over the magnification glasses and said, "I'm better at stitching than I am at this part."

Charlie said, "Will I be able to work?"

"Sure. In a few days. No tendons cut."

"Good." A few days to Charlie meant tomorrow.

"Glad you punched a mirror instead of whoever you got this mad at. Fixing broken jaws is even harder than picking glass out of someone's hand."

"Yeah."

"The other guy's jaw, of course. You'd have put him away."

Charlie didn't say anything.

While Dr. Spinelli stitched, he said, "They got doctors for anger, too, these days."

Charlie didn't say anything.

"Tough being a fireman. Tough job."

When he left, Charlie said, "I'll tell it to you, Margie. Just to you. I need you."

She reached over and patted his wrist above the bandages. "Okay. But I'm going to tape all the windows. Like in a hurricane."

He smiled across the table at her, though he tried to hide his gratitude so as not to pressure her. But he did say, "I don't want to lose you," because he couldn't help but be honest. That was his nature.

"I know," Margie said.

"I'm sorry we haven't had a normal life."

And now it was Margie's turn to remain silent. He waited. He said, "Can we talk at the beach? Can we rent a cottage at the beach for a week?"

"I'd love to."

"You can read a lot."

"Yes."

"We can go make love at the creek."

"I don't know about that."

"Why not?"

"A little chilly in October."

His weary eyes crinkled at the corners. "No mosquitoes, though."

"There's those new condos. If people look out the windows and see us screwing in their view of the marsh grass, they might not enjoy their dinner."

They smirked at one another.

The sand dune was building up again. And besides the condominiums behind the creek, Margie and Charlie found another change—a little metal bridge crossing the creek so that the condo owners could get to the beach. If a small boat wanted to sail up the creek, the sailor had to get out and hand crank the bridge up, like a toy drawbridge. Margie thought the bridge was cute. Charlie wondered how the bridge got by the environmentalists. They tried the bridge and it worked. They cranked it up and down and up and down.

"Convenient, at least," he said.

"Yeah."

Before, you could only cross the creek at low tide. As children, Little Pete and Margie used to enter the creek at high tide, holding their crab nets and lines and towels and Margie's library books above their heads, making believe they were marines crossing leech-infested swamps. Margie remembered the time she dropped *A Tree Grows in Brooklyn* into the creek, but Little Pete deftly retrieved it with his crab net. Even though Margie had dried it in the sun, the librarian still made Margie pay for it. The woman picked it up with her thumb and forefinger, held it for a dramatic second over her wastebasket, and let it drop. So Margie took out her money, paid the bill, and asked her if she could keep the book. The librarian rolled her eyes, and *A Tree Grows in Brooklyn* was liberated for the second time.

On the other side of the bridge, once they'd settled down on their blanket, Margie told Charlie she wanted a separation. He said, "Where do you want to separate to?" He didn't feign shock at what he'd known was coming. He wasn't panicked either.

She said, "Radcliffe."

He smiled sadly. "Then it's more than a separation you want."

"Yes. I want to start up again where I stopped."

"You'll never want to get back into the horseradish."

"That's right."

He turned on to his side. Margie was on her back. He looked down into her eyes. "But that's where I'll be."

She turned to him, too, face-to-face. "Your choice," she said.

He said, "I have no choice."

"Yes, you do."

"Help me."

Margie touched him. "Just talk to me, Charlie, the way I talked to you when we were lying right here such a long time ago. Now it's your turn."

First he played with a strand of her hair. Then he said,

"The alternative to my being out of the horseradish is different than the one you see for yourself."

"Charlie. Tell me what it is you see for yourself."

"All I see is losing you. Same as if I stay in the jar. So why make an effort?"

"Oh, great. You cop out." She ran her fingers against his lips. "Charlie, I don't have much patience left."

"I know."

"Giving up what I need—what I'm telling you I have to have—if I give it up, that won't help you."

"I'm not asking for that."

"I know. But you can't go around totaling mirrors."

He sighed. "Why did you pick Radcliffe? Was that the result of a consultation with Martha?"

Margie made a fist and tapped his chin. "You know, I'm getting a little tired of poor Martha taking the blame every time I blink. No, it wasn't Martha."

"Well, then?"

"Well, the thing about reading the *New York Times* every day is that you get these little gossip columns of information on the lives of the rich and intellectual."

"So what did the *Times* say about Radcliffe?"

"Radcliffe feels that applicants should all be treated alike. That accepted freshmen should be treated alike. If you're fifty years old and you get in, you get to room in a dorm like everyone else."

"A freshman just like all the eighteen-year-olds."

"That's right."

"Will you come home for Thanksgiving?"

"I wouldn't miss your mother's Thanksgiving dinner for all the tea in Radcliffe."

Charlie lay back and pulled her onto him. "Margie, if Radcliffe was in Pennsylvania instead of a stone's throw from Fenway Park, would you still want to go?"

"Nope."

He pulled her head down against his chest. During that hug Charlie was giving her, Margie made a decision. If he asked whether he could come visit her at Radcliffe, she would divorce him. If he didn't, she wouldn't. Margie waited. He didn't ask. She pulled up from him—her turn to look down into his eyes. His eyelashes fluttered against the sun behind her. Margie said, "I love you."

He said, "I love you."

Then he kissed her and then he whispered in her ear, "I want you."

Margie said, "I want you."

Badly. Her terms were not subject to compromise any-more, and he knew it. He didn't ask for one. It was time for all-out comfort, temporary though that comfort would be. As they moved their blanket into the marsh grass, Margie was thinking that sex was the same as what the doctor in "Star Trek" did to injured crew members—touched them where it hurt, creating some kind of orgasm where the injured parts knit themselves back together and everything was okay till the next injury came along.

It was fairly warm for October, Margie thought. And the people in the condominiums be damned.

Chapter Seventeen

Charlie dismantled the war room. He steamed the circus mural off the wall. He donated all his notebooks and tapes to the Hartford Historical Society. Then, because he loved Margie so much, he gave her a room to please her most fanciful daydreams. He took up the carpet and sanded the oak floors and stained them. He bought two small Chinese rugs. He put up some sort of flocked wallpaper imported from England, and mahogany wainscoting he'd found at a house-wrecking company's yard. Then he went all through the house and collected her books from various shelves in every room: from the coffee table, too; from the end tables; from the bedroom floor on her side of the bed; from under the bed; from her bureau; from the bathroom; from the kitchen counter.

He filled the stained and oiled and polished shelves with all

Margie's books, arranging them alphabetically by title. Margie never connected writers specifically to the books they wrote, so that was okay. He put a print of her favorite painting on the wall, the Fragonard of the woman reading in the sunlight. He had knocked out the little window in the room and put in a bigger one so that Margie could read by sunlight, too, just like the woman in the painting. He even bought a small bench with a tapestry cushion so she could *be* the woman in the painting. There was a wing chair and a leather sofa, and a brass table from India. The room looked like one big, cozy nook. A personalized library of Margie's own.

There was a little shelf for the catalogs from Trinity College in Hartford, and Wesleyan down the road in Middletown, and UCONN and the University of Hartford. Margie didn't really want to go away to college. She'd go to one right nearby and find out what authors try to tell people about human nature.

When it was finished, Margie sat in the leather wing chair and looked around at her present. Charlie had basically adapted the design of the room where Alistair Cooke introduced "Masterpiece Theatre." Alistair was gone and Public Television had redesigned his room. Fans, Margie thought, would be happy to know that the original still existed.

It was the loveliest present Margie could imagine, and the day that the room was officially unveiled, she found out who set fire to the Barnum & Bailey circus tent on July 6, 1944. He finally confessed, and included details demonstrating that Henry Maxson had told the truth.

The confession came just a few weeks before Charlie's six-month ultimatum was to expire. It happened right when Margie threw her library-warming party. It was winter then, between Thanksgiving and Christmas, and Margie had tried to re-create Dickens—she served mulled wine and mince pie with hard sauce to all the family milling about the leather furniture and tapestry cushions, all raving about what a beautiful room it was and how Charlie had missed his calling. Someone actually said that: He missed his calling. Margie looked to Martha, who never could fathom how or why her father had missed his whole life. Like her grandfather. Charlie's cousin Cindy was the last to arrive; she came in just when things were on the verge of breaking up. She was such a contrast to all of them. They had rosy cheeks from the wine and from the toastiness of the room. Cindy's skin was always pale. She was alone. A pretty girl, everyone had always said, which meant: Why isn't she married? And since she wasn't, she was still referred to as a girl.

Martha went right over to her and the two went off and chatted in a corner. In deference to Cindy, the party seemed to just start up again. Margie was glad; she was enjoying herself. She was proud of Charlie. He was going to be all right.

People began re-eating. "This stuff on the pie is delicious, Margie," was what people kept saying.

Then Margie felt Martha's eyes on her. Margie looked back at her, at her daughter's wide, wet eyes. Martha's face was bone white, whiter than Cindy's. She was standing by Cindy, who was sitting on the tapestry bench under the big window. Martha had one of Cindy's hands enclosed in both of hers, holding it up against her stomach. Margie walked over to them, and when she reached them, Martha said, "Excuse me," and tried to escape, but Cindy held fast to her. In Charlie's family of extrasensory perception, everybody seemed to turn toward them at once.

Cindy mumbled something. She mumbled, "Aunt Palma."

And another tide of just perceptible turning took place and Margie's mother-in-law's eyes shifted, searching out the wrath of her husband. Then she remembered she was safe, and stiffened, and shot a look at Cindy, a look Margie had never seen. A dangerous look, a direct physical threat. Martha pulled Cindy's hand up higher to her chest and gazed down into her eyes, a gesture that served to release Cindy from Palma's horrible gaze. Now Martha held on to Cindy's gaze until, slowly, Cindy's head turned and she looked at Margie. She said, "Margie, my Aunt Palma wouldn't let me tell. But now it's over so I will. I did see something at the circus." Her gaze moved toward Charlie, who was standing on the other side of the room, and everyone else looked to him, too. Margie thought his face seemed wizened, creased with lines that had never been there before. Cindy said to Charlie, her voice awry, "I saw you. I waved, but you didn't see me. Near where we were going in. You were standing on the other side of the animal chute." She gave a sad little smile. "I was so glad you'd gotten to go to the circus after all. When we went to your house . . . after . . . I told Aunt Palma that I'd seen you there. She said I shouldn't tell or Uncle Denny would beat you to death. But I already knew that, that's why I didn't tell my mother you were there."

Then Margie watched Charlie shrink. She couldn't comprehend that he wasn't actually shrinking, that instead he was sinking to his knees, sinking in slow motion until finally he became the same size he was when he was ten years old. When he set the circus tent on fire.

Palma O'Neill was the only one who had actually recognized that Charlie had set the fire. When Cindy whispered her words to Palma a long time ago she had known. She had put Cindy's words together with Charlie appearing at the door in such a terrible state—sweaty and in shock. She realized the shock had not come from the fear of having to face his father for not putting out the garbage, which was why his father had taken the ticket away. But as Palma had already tried to explain to Margie, she was of a generation that considered the expression of feelings a weakness and the hiding of those feelings acceptable. She didn't see where that phenomenon became hiding the truth, became lying, which Margie had euphemized as not being frank. Became betrayal.

And then Margie saw everything—all of it—through Palma's eyes: Denny isn't really hurting the children, my brothers would kill him if he were; the children aren't angry and bitter and resentful; after all, what do kids know? My husband is a bad man, but he's not so bad that he'd drive my child to put a match to a circus tent full of people, full of other children. Palma was able to believe her own lies.

At the moment of revelation, when Charlie sank to the floor of the library he'd built so painstakingly for Margie, Martha had to desert Cindy and take hold of her mother—hold her back by her shoulders. She held her back that day, and in the days to follow. When she got her put and could trust Margie not to attack whoever might be in her path, she spent her time traveling back and forth across the house, back and forth between her father and mother. Charlie was in his sickbed in the bedroom. "Mental collapse" was how Martha described it to everyone who asked. She told Margie that, too. Margie said to her: "I don't give a shit."

Margie slept in Martha's room with her. Charlie's family kept coming to visit, one by one. Margie refused to see any of them. Except Cindy.

Cindy and Martha and Margie sat on Margie's bed like the girls in the dorm at Radcliffe. Cindy said, "Margie, Aunt Palma said if I told, Uncle Denny would beat Charlie to death." Cindy wanted to be sure Margie knew that those were the exact words. She hadn't said he'd spank Charlie. She'd said he'd beat him to death. Cindy, at five, knew what a spanking from Denny meant. She'd witnessed them. Poor thing. So it was weak little Cindy who gave Margie the strength to imagine speaking to Charlie, another poor thing. Cindy was the one who got Margie past being too filled with fury to function. Palma had sacrificed her granddaughter to the lie. And Chick, if he suspected, and how could he not, thought he was protecting his nephew from himself. The truth, after all, would eventually disappear. But it hadn't. Just as it hadn't for little Bobby Corcoran.

It was Martha who made her mother see that Charlie had wanted one thing from Margie for all the years that they were married—that she read his mind, the mind he couldn't read himself. But she'd refused. She hadn't wanted to ruin a good and thrilling book. And now Martha worked and worked to make her mother understand that Charlie never lied to her. That he didn't know what he'd done. That he really did suppress the memory. Until he was jolted. By Margie's threatening to leave. That's what got him to stop after all.

Margie broke. First she said, "Martha, I need your help. You're giving up on me. You're resenting me."

Now Martha could aim her big guns. She'd been waiting for Margie to signal the moment. Her brief was ready and set to go. She spoke the way she was being taught to speak to her future clients; you give them the big speech the moment they first begin to see straight. Before they can start lying to themselves.

"Mom, Daddy is finally able to face what he'd done. He gave up the search that night in the library because somewhere inside him, he knew he'd be able to cope with what really happened. If that wasn't so, he would have made a joke about what Cindy said at the party. He would have allowed Chick to change the subject. But he didn't. I don't know what you've been pounding him with these last few months, but it worked. You did it."

Before Margie walked down the hall to visit Charlie, she said to Martha, "Who's going to get poor Cindy back?"

Martha said, "Cindy will get herself back, I'd say. She's been released, Mom."

"Released. They were all released."

"Mom?"

"What honey?"

"Mom, I don't want you to think I'm not still caring, here, because I am. But I've been wanting to tell you something. Can I tell you something about me?"

"Oh, Martha, what's wrong?"

"No, no, nothing's wrong. In fact, something's right, believe it or not."

"Thank God for that."

"Remember the guy I told you about? Richard?"

Margie thought, Richard, Richard.

"I miss him. I'm going to get married."

Martha's smile was crooked because Martha, who could smile for four people, had gotten out of practice. Margie put her arms out to her. Martha snuggled up to her mother, lay her head on her shoulder. Margie said, "I'm so glad, baby."

Martha pulled back and her real smile was back. "Guess what else?"

"What, honey?"

"He's Jewish, Mom. Just like us."

The first thing Margie said to Charlie after Martha had gone was, "A ten-year-old cannot contain the kind of anger that you had been forced to hold inside. Children aren't supposed to even know about that kind of anger." She was standing next to his bed in the darkened room.

He didn't say anything. She knew he didn't want pity from her or anyone else. He wanted punishment. He wanted his father to beat him to death. But all the same, he was piteous.

So then Margie said, "Tell me what happened."

He didn't say anything.

She sat down on the edge of the bed. She said, "I'll be you, Charlie, and you be one of the people who comes to see the fireman to tell him what he witnessed at the circus on the day of the fire." Margie sat up straight. "Okay, now I'm you, and you're the witness. Here goes. . . ." She cleared her throat. "What happened on the day you went to the circus?"

He said, "Margie."

She said, "Tell me! It's time to tell so that you can start getting into all this forgiveness bullshit that everyone expects from each other these days. Jesus, Charlie, if one more person says to me that you've got to forgive your father before you can heal yourself, I'm going to go buy a gun and shoot him."

"I'll never forgive him."

"That's right. Why should you? He never wanted forgiveness because he never saw himself as evil. To him, your mother was some kind of sport—target practice. Denny O'Neill didn't give a shit about you so now you don't have to worry about not giving a shit about him. But Charlie, here's what I think. It's time to say that you'll never forgive your mother."

He said, "My mother is a saint."

And Margie took out her big guns. "A mother is supposed to protect you, same as a father, right? She didn't. But any good that might come out of this is that maybe she'll ask your forgiveness. Maybe she'll repent. Then you'll be able to forgive her. That's when it makes sense to forgive—when the other person asks for forgiveness. Because then she'll be saying that you're not the one at fault here. And you're not."

"Margie, my mother . . ."

"Okay, forget your mother. What about Bob Corcoran? Something triggered him and now something triggered you. Me. I triggered you. It took me a goddamn long time. I'm sorry, Charlie. Will you forgive me?"

Charlie finally looked into Margie's eyes. He swallowed. His look became hard instead of piteous. He said, "You refused to see what you were seeing. You saw heartache, Margie, and you made believe it was a game."

"No," she said, "a book. I saw a book. A goddamn book. I said I'm sorry." Margie put her face into her hands and tried to keep herself from sobbing, but she couldn't, so she sobbed and babbled to him. "A long time ago, Charlie, you found someone who you thought would get you out of that pit your father threw you into. But I failed you. I'm sorry, Charlie. I'm sorry."

He didn't touch her and he wouldn't let himself comfort her, though that was all he wanted to do. He was waiting to see what decision she'd made. She was going to do something and he had to wait and find out what it was.

Margie got up and left the room. She went into Martha's room and she got a cassette and a recorder. She came back, put in the cassette, turned on the recorder, and the tape began to go around. She said, "Charlie. Tell me everything that you remember about the circus. The matinee performance of the Barnum & Bailey circus in Hartford, Connecticut, on July sixth, nineteen forty-four."

He said, "I remember everything."

Margie said, "Begin at an appropriate time."

He closed his eyes. She waited. Then he said, "I was so excited, I couldn't sleep all night." Several witnesses had said that very same thing. And then they'd stop and Charlie would prod them.

So Margie said, "Go on."

"Uncle Chick had chosen me of all the kids. I was really going to the circus. And with Aunt Annette, who would buy me a souvenir. Aunt Annette would always buy me ice cream when the ice-cream man came. She'd never say, 'We've got a box of Popsicles in the fridge.' That's what my mother would say since my father wouldn't let her buy me an ice cream. I was going to the circus with my two cousins and my best aunt. Mama put out my lightest shirt because it was going to be such a hot day. She laid the shirt on the end of the bed along with my blue shorts. I remember finally shutting my eyes when the birds started singing. So I didn't wake up until ten.

"Uncle Chick picked me up in his police car after lunch. He was in his uniform on his way to work. Aunt Annette and the girls were in the back so I could ride in the front seat. He let me hit the siren once. Then he left us at the bus stop. I had to hold hands with Cindy. Ruth-Ann held her hand on the other side. I didn't have a little sister. I felt proud to be doing my share to take care of her. My father came while we were waiting for the bus. He smiled at me. As soon as he smiled, I knew I wasn't going to the circus.

"Aunt Annette said: 'Hi, Denny.' The girls said: 'Hello, Uncle Denny.' But he never took his eyes off me. He said: 'Hear you slept late this morning, son.' And I said: 'Yes, sir.' He said: 'Your mother had to take out the garbage. Is that right, son?'

"I'd never thought once about the garbage. I'd gotten up so late. He said again: 'Is that right, son?' I said: 'Yes, sir.' And he asked me if that wasn't my chore, which it was. Then he said: 'And when you don't do your chores, what happens?' And I said: 'I get punished.' He asked me what I thought my punishment should be. He always asked. He usually asked my mother. I told him I didn't know. This was the one time I knew. That's why he said: 'I think you do, son.' Then he said: '*Son?*' And he kept saying: '*Son? Son? Son?*' Then he screamed, '*Son!*' into my ear. The girls were squashed together, hiding behind Aunt Annette. Aunt Annette tried to say something, but he was bent to my ear. He hissed into my face; he said: 'You get your skinny little ass home right now, and I don't want to look at your fucking puss for the rest of the day. I'll see you tonight, when I get home.' And then he smiled again. His face was right up to mine. He said: 'Give me your ticket.' I knew that's what he'd say."

Charlie stopped talking. He was staring up at the ceiling. Margie couldn't let him stop, even though she wished she could stop breathing, could commit *suttee*. So she asked him if he'd like a glass of water just like he asked all the witnesses.

He told her he'd like some orange juice. Charlie loved orange juice with ice. All firemen do. Nothing else wipes out the taste of soot so well.

When she came back, she handed him the orange juice and asked, "Then what happened?"

"I ran home. I was hot and sweaty even before I started to run. I ran through the backyards, past the library, and instead of crossing over the stream, I ran down into it. There was no water. The water had dried up. I climbed into the culvert. It was cool and dark in the culvert. I used to go there a lot in the summertime.

"Then I heard the bus go by. I waited a few minutes, and then I climbed out. My mother would cry when I got back home. I tried to think about waiting a few hours and then going home and making believe I'd been to the circus. But she'd find out the truth anyway. I walked up the hill, down the street, and then I saw another bus coming. My mother had given me a quarter for cotton candy. I ran back to the corner, the bus came and stopped for me, and I got on. I told the bus driver I was going to the circus. He said, 'Aren't you the lucky one?' He handed me a transfer. I asked him what bus I had to take next.

"He said: 'Get off at Main Street in front of the Loew's Poli, and take the Bloomfield Avenue bus. Only have to wait five minutes. Don't worry,' he told me, 'you got plenty of time.' When I got off at Main, he said: 'Have a swell time, kid.'

"And I kept thinking that I wasn't going to have a swell time because my father took my ticket. I kept thinking that even though I wasn't going to have a swell time, Ruth-Ann would. Ruth-Ann was a snotty kid, always in trouble. But she was going to the circus all the same. And I wasn't. I always tried to be good, but I didn't know how to be good. I couldn't figure out how to be good. So I wasn't going."

He stopped. He was sweating just like he'd been sweating

on that humid July day. Margie was as cold as ice. She said, "What did you do?"

He said, "I killed your mother and I nearly killed you."

Margie hung on. "My mother would have been the first person to forgive you. You've repented. You've devoted your life to repenting to her. She would have forgiven you."

"And what about you?"

"Charlie. Please tell me that you can see I've forgiven you."

"Margie . . ."

"Wait. I need to get back to where we were. What did you do when the bus left you off?"

He reached out and brushed at her arm. "Your voice sounds like mine, Margie, when I asked people."

"Is it any wonder? Just tell me, Charlie. It's my turn to need to know."

He took his eyes from her. He sipped his juice. He said, "I walked down from the bus stop at the corner of Barbour Street. I walked all the way around the lot. The circus tent was beautiful, flags flying everywhere. Thousands of people were milling around the tent. There's such a mystery about a circus tent, Margie. Because there are no windows to peek through. And inside, where you can't see, you know there's danger. No nets. It's human nature to love danger when there isn't a threat to you. No threat." Margie placed her hand on his forearm. It was slippery. Across his knuckles, his own scars, the ones from the broken mirror, were still pink.

"So I watched everyone go in. I never spotted Aunt Annette or the girls. I was watching out for them, but I didn't see them." He looked over at Margie. "Cindy saw me."

"Yes."

"I never knew it. I never knew it till the party."

"Your mother knew it."

"Yes."

Margie removed her hand from his arm. "I wonder if Cindy will ever forgive her."

His eyes filled with agony at the exposure of the martyred saint. "Please, Margie."

"What happened next, Charlie?"

"I saw a book of matches on the ground."

Margie swallowed back the gagging reflex. So did Charlie.

"I stared at them and then I picked them up and put them in my pocket. I walked around the tent. The roustabouts were backing the animal trailers up to the chute. The music started inside the tent. I got to watch the animals run through the chute. Then they were inside. There was a real hot breeze that kept coming up. Papers were blowing around. I picked up some crumpled newspaper pages. When the animals started running back out of the tent, I took the matches out and I lit the papers. I held the papers to the bottom of the tent, but the wind came up again and blew pieces of the burning papers up over my head and against the tent. The tent caught fire in a dozen places, maybe more. In one place, it got to be a big circle of fire. It grew bigger and bigger. No one came to put it out. I turned around and ran to the edge of the lot. I heard the fire before I saw it. I heard the freight-train roar that a fire makes when it sucks up oxygen."

And Margie thought about the inside of the tent where the people were hearing the music that Merle Evans played with the volume turned up as high as the bandleader could get it. Margie wasn't conscious of Charlie's weeping. She had no idea he was weeping until she looked at him.

She brought out the cannon. "When you lit the newspaper, what did you think would happen?"

He took several long, deep breaths. He said, "Margie. I thought the tent would catch fire, what else could I think? What would a ten-year-old think?"

"Yes. That is what a ten-year-old would think. But what else would he think? What did you think would happen after the tent caught fire?"

His eyes grew focused over Margie's head, back to a scene

in 1944. He put himself back there one last time. "I thought it would be like a fire drill at school. Everyone would file out. But since this was a real fire, and not a drill, the firemen would come."

"Then what would happen? When the firemen came?"

"They'd put the fire out."

"You set a fire you knew the firemen would put out."

"Yes."

"Why?"

"Because they'd have to cancel the circus for that day. Everybody would miss out, just like I had to miss out. Even that brat, Ruth-Ann."

There was just silence. Then Margie said, "Your father caused the fire. Your mother caused it, too, as if she struck the match herself." The room became silent again. He didn't get angry. Charlie reached over and took Margie's hand. His voice stayed a little boy's. "I thought the firemen would put it out."

Margie said, "I know."

She took off her sneakers and climbed into bed with him. She snuggled up to him. They made love.

Charlie would be the one to get Margie out of the jar of horseradish. Not Martha, not Radcliffe, not a million books. Charlie. He'd pull her out—the little girl who wouldn't have plastic surgery, who had refused and refused. The teenager who wouldn't go to college, wouldn't go anywhere, just like her father. The woman who just wanted to make sure everyone saw what they'd done to her. Fuck you, Miss Foss, and fuck everybody else. Look what you people did to me!

Now Charlie was finally able to read her mind.

AFTERWORD

The backdrop of this novel, the great Hartford circus fire, was a real event. And the unidentified child who was known as Little Miss 1565 was a victim of that fire. In 1991, after an intensive nine-year search, a Hartford firefighter, Lt. Rick Davy, discovered the identity of that child. Her name was Eleanor Cook.

Of the 169 people who died in the fire, there remain six who have yet to be identified, including an infant, less than a year old.

ABOUT THE AUTHOR

Mary-Ann Tirone Smith grew up in Hartford, Connecticut.